SHADOWFALL

SHADOWS BOOK ONE

TW IAIN

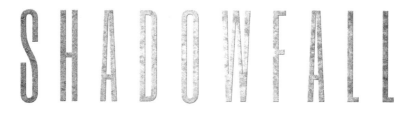

Cover design by Deranged Doctor Design
www.derangeddoctordesign.com

Visit www.twiain.com for more information

SHADOWS

Shadowfall (Book One)
Shadowsiege (Book Two)
Shadowstrike (Book Three)

Shadowlair (A Shadows Prequel)—Mailing list exclusive novella

DOMINIONS

Dark Glass (Dominions I)
Dead Flesh (Dominions II)
Deep Water (Dominions III)
Riled Dogs (Dominions IV)
Rogue Wolf (Dominions V)
Rebel Rout (Dominions VI)
Fading Control (Dominions VII)
Fallen Domain (Dominions VIII)
Final Target (Dominions IX)

Gatekeeper (A Dominions Prologue)
Control (A Dominions Story)—Mailing list exclusive novella
Expedient (A Dominions Story)
Animus (A Dominions Story)
Errant (A Dominions Story)
Impact (A Dominions Story)

The hunger was never far away.

The creature had fed recently, back in one of the other caves. It had opened the wound and sucked eagerly, taking in as much as it could. Others had been waiting for their turn, and it would have fought them if they approached. But they didn't interrupt. They knew it needed the energy, for what it was about to do.

But the food supply was tainted, the source already weakened. And that was why the creature pushed through the caves, so dark and cold and perfect. That was why the creature explored.

They needed more food.

The creature moved through the blackness with ease, and even when the tunnel fell away, the creature climbed as fast as it walked.

The tunnel opened into a cave. The air was different, rich with the smell of vegetation, and it blew cool against the creature's hide. The darkness was no longer all-consuming, and the creature hesitated. But it took a step forward anyway. The shadows allowed that much.

It sniffed, and turned its attention to the outside. The atmosphere was heavy with moisture, but it sensed life, far below. That would be the large forest creatures. They would do in an emergency, but their blood was sickly, and the energy it gave was short-lived.

But there was another trace rising from the forest, and although it was distant, the scent was familiar. It rekindled the hunger, and the creature salivated.

A fresh supply of food approached, and that excited the creature almost to distraction. It yearned to sink its fangs into flesh. It craved the sharp, bitter taste hitting the back of its throat. It relished the feeling of power that would cascade through its body.

It inched closer to the opening of the cave, and could have climbed down. The clouds were heavy, and the trees were tall enough to provide shelter if they could be reached with speed. But it knew the benefits of patience. It knew about stealth. It wasn't some dumb animal, like the large forest beasts.

And so it retreated, back into the shadows. And it waited.

ONE

The Proteus lurched to starboard, and the seat restraints bit into Brice's shoulders. Again.

"How we holding up, Keelin?" Cathal asked, from his seat at the back of the bridge. If Brice turned to look at his commander, he knew the face would be as emotionless as the voice.

"Not enjoying this," Keelin said as she rolled the craft to starboard. Brice switched his lenses to the internal sensor and saw her grimace, glazed eyes half hidden by strands of hair. Her hands curled round the ends of the armrests in concentration.

"How long?"

"An hour plus." There was a whine from the engines. "Plus a lot, the way this storm's growing."

Over an hour stuck to his chair on this rust-bucket. Brice couldn't wait to get back to Haven.

"You finished your report yet, Brice?"

"Almost."

"No time like the present."

Brice nodded. The others had probably finished ages ago, reports all filed and ready for collation. But Brice hadn't even started, and Cathal must know that. But what could he add?

He pulled the file up through his lattice, the blank page filling his lenses. He stared at it for a moment, then recorded the bare facts. Fly out, land next to the abandoned Proteus. Start investigation, but nothing of interest on the craft besides a removed panel. No clear reason for this. Ryann tracked the missing crew into the forest, up to the edge of the gully. The trail headed down, following a line of bolts. There was no rope. Ryann said she couldn't detect anyone nearby.

Cathal called the search off. With the increasing storm, climbing down was a risk he was unprepared to take. They returned to their own Proteus, and headed home.

Tris moaned about being cold and wet the whole time, of course. Brice was tempted to put that in his report, but he knew Cathal would remove it. He'd say the company wasn't interested in such pettiness, but Brice knew it would reflect poorly on Cathal himself. It wouldn't do for a commander to have dissension in the ranks.

The company had an image to uphold, after all.

"Tris, you patched in?" asked Cathal.

As crew tech, Tris sat next to the pilot—some hold-over from ancient times, apparently. Of course, Tris could work from anywhere through his lattice, and there was no need for him to sit up front. All it did was stroke his ego.

Tris swivelled his chair to face Cathal, and ran a hand over the clumps of hair he called a beard. "Signal reach to Haven's fluctuating between six and ten bars. I've tried routing through freq-mod, but atmos gamma's running at seventeen per, so that's a no-go."

Typical data-drivel. Brice snorted. "You mean you can't reach Haven?"

"Think you could do any better?" Tris' jaw clenched, and he tried to look imposing. Brice wanted to laugh.

"Keep it civil, boys," said Cathal, stern but bored. "Tris, keep trying. Brice, if you've finished your report, send it to Ryann."

"Sending now."

He had the file on auto-push anyway. He re-read the few sparse sentences, decided it would do, and signed off. His lattice pinged when Ryann received it.

"Thanks," she said, her voice as soft as usual, and Brice gave her a nod. She sat in the chair across from him, her eyes glazed and her face serene.

Brice still wasn't sure what to make of the crew's second-in-command. She was one of the best trackers on Haven, a trained medic, and everyone spoke highly of her. But she seemed distant, like everything she said was planned. She seemed to care, but the emotion felt too forced.

"Tris, try hold-out seventeen," she said. "It's in use. Might be close enough to relay our signal."

"On it. Nyle Patera and Osker Rella. Just the two of them?"

"Training mission."

"Right."

Brice envied Nyle and Osker. The hold-outs were little more than concrete blocks, but they beat being stuck in a Proteus in a storm.

The Proteus shuddered and dropped, and Brice's stomach lurched.

"That trees we're hitting, Keelin?" Tris said.

"Only the tops. This baby can take it."

"You sure?"

As if a tech could do better than a pilot, Brice thought.

"I know what I'm doing. Just need to find somewhere to drop into the basin."

"Thought we were running the rim. That was the plan, right?"

"Storm's changed that."

"Anywhere to drop?" Cathal asked. Brice wondered why he didn't pull up the maps himself. But why should he do any work when he had a crew to do it for him?

"Closest possibility's the Tumbler."

Of all the waterfalls cascading into the basin, the Tumbler was the biggest. And the most powerful. Brice had read of the drone, the one that crashed last year. A sudden down-draft slammed it into the vertical water, and it disappeared. They said parts of it were still churning round in the plunge-pool's maelstrom.

But something about air pressure made waterfalls ideal drop-points. Or was it thermals? Some technical garbage, anyway. The kind of stuff Tris would get all excited by.

"Your call, Keelin," Cathal said, and it annoyed Brice that he was off-loading the decision. "And take a break if you need it."

"Prefer to get back as soon as."

"And I'd prefer to get back in one piece."

The Proteus tilted gently to starboard, and the engines whined. Brice sighed, and linked to the external sensors.

His lenses flared up as lightning streaked across the sky, and he felt more than heard the deep boom of the thunder. The heavy clouds were dark, and rain lashed down onto the forest canopy. The wind roared through the trees, and to Brice the forest looked like an angry sea, waiting to devour them.

Ahead, he saw a line snaking through the trees, and he knew this was the Tumbler's feeder river. The line grew as they approached.

He tuned in to the haptic sensors, and his skin prickled with the cold harshness of the air, and the rain stung like a thousand angry insects. But there was also warmth in the friction of the air rushing over the Proteus' hull.

The craft clipped the tree-tops, and raked across his belly. He winced, but then he thought how much more intense this would be for Keelin. She was locked in to every sensor, truly at one with her craft. In some senses, she was the Proteus. To move it, she merely had to think.

The craft jerked, and Brice's head was tossed to one side, his body held in place by the seat restraints. It was enough to pull him from the sensors.

"You okay, green?" There was a hint of a smile on Cathal's stubbled face.

"Fine," Brice said. He hated it when Cathal called him green. He never used that term for Tris or Keelin, even though they'd only joined the crew a week before he'd signed up.

<Don't mind him, Brice,> Ryann sussed, her lattice reaching for his and placing her words directly into his mind. *<Get to his age, and everyone's green.>*

"Taking us down," Keelin said.

Brice locked on to the outside sensors again as the Proteus dropped towards the water. The river flowed so fast and steadily that it appeared to be a solid thing, and he almost imagined Keelin would land on that surface. But she stopped a couple of metres above it, setting the craft to hover, facing a line where the river stopped and the sky began.

To either side of them, the river tore through the trees, ripping branches free, dragging trunks from their roots. It dragged the debris to the lip of the waterfall, and then threw it down, to be reduced to splinters by the churning waters below.

Brice pulled out. Hovering over the water made him feel queasy.

"Tris, any joy with the hold-out?" Cathal asked.

Tris shook his head. "Can't pull enough power into the boosters."

"That's me," Keelin said. "Need to keep the Proteus steady. Just give me a moment."

Tris didn't respond, and Brice knew he was annoyed. But Keelin outranked him. Everyone outranked Tris, apart from Brice.

He was the crew's grunt. That wasn't the official role, obviously, but that was what they called him, often to his face. His lattice was tweaked for physical enhancements, and so he did the heavy lifting. He did all the donkey work.

"Take as long as you need, Keelin," Cathal said. "Prefer to get back late than not at all."

And then the lights flickered. They turned off for a second, and when they came back on, they cast a dim glow.

"Great!" muttered Keelin. "They were supposed to have fixed this."

"Glich?" asked Tris.

"More like a screw-up. Odd times, we stay stationary for more than a minute, the Proteus thinks we're parked and cuts to minimal power."

"Can't you over-ride it?"

Keelin turned her head to Tris. "Right," she drawled. "Never thought of that."

"I'll speak to Arela again," Ryann said, before Tris formed a come-back.

"Can't see that helping, but thanks anyway," said Keelin.

Arela Angelis. Brice had only met Haven's chief commander a couple of times. The woman was fierce, and acted like she was independent, but they all knew she was under the thumb of the company. Kaiahive—so big it controlled governments, so big it dealt in everything from food processing to mining to high-tech development. So important it was the only company that offered superior lattice tweaking, unless you went black-market and risked a total melt-down.

And so self-important that it only spent the bare minimum. It was no wonder the name was rarely mentioned. They were 'the company', and they screwed everyone over. They didn't give the refit guys the parts they needed, and insisted they make do. They forced Keelin's baby to hobble on with problems patched over, the plasters peeling away at the slightest disturbance, but they'd complain if missions were not a success.

Arela might be able to pull a few strings, but she wouldn't stick her neck out too far, and they all knew it.

The lights flickered again.

"Tris, help run diagnostic," Keelin said.

"On it."

Silence descended on the bridge. Everyone had their eyes down as they retreated into their lattices, pulling up data or rifling through reports. Brice shrugged, and plugged into the craft's systems once more.

Nothing was ideal. If he stayed in the bridge, the grey walls felt oppressive. But if he connected with the sensors, and saw the world outside, it only reminded him that he was stuck on the craft.

He looked to the trees, longing to be amongst them, even in this weather. The leaves were thick, and they'd keep off most of the rain. The wind wouldn't penetrate too badly, either.

There were the warths, of course, but Ryann would sense them, and would guide the crew around the beasts. They were only a danger when provoked, anyway.

The Proteus vibrated, and Brice felt the wind pushing down on them, funnelled by the trees. The water churned below, and Brice followed its flow, towards the line that stretched out, where the river ended and the clouds began. A branch—no, a fallen tree—was swept past, and it teetered on the edge for a moment before disappearing from view. Maybe he could hear the roar of the Tumbler. Or maybe that was the thunder that constantly rumbled.

And then the sky burst open with lightning.

Brice saw it in a negative freeze-frame, the trees suddenly brilliant white, before the intensity slammed into him. White-hot pain shot through his body, pulling every muscle rigid. His heart stuttered and his lungs squeezed.

The Proteus twisted and fell.

Two

Ryann felt everything.

The moment the lightning struck—because that surely was what had happened—her lattice switched to hyper-sensitivity. The illusion of time slowed as she analysed all inputs.

The Proteus slammed into the water. It twisted, almost lazily, and the engines spluttered. Keelin cried out inside. Ryann felt her mind shift as she dived into the craft's controls. Tris flared with anger and panic. He wasn't controlling his adrenaline, but letting it consume him.

<Tris, work on power. Help Keelin,> she sussed, giving him the distraction he needed.

Cathal's heart-rate jumped, but he forced a barrier up, sealing his emotions until later.

The craft tilted to port, a down-draft pushing from the stern. They faced up-stream, and Ryann saw the water push the Proteus' nose, forcing them towards the waterfall.

Brice was dark, and that was a concern. When Ryann pushed, there was only the suggestion of a lattice. It was like trying to grab at mist.

The hull creaked as their nose lifted, water forcing the Proteus upright. She dug into the data, and read how their stern was trapped against a tangle of rock and a web of wood. The river pushed them vertical, and for a second they teetered, the craft groaning in complaint.

And then they fell.

The seat restraints pinned Ryann in place, and for a moment she was weightless. Then, the Proteus spinning, pressure drove into her chest, and a roar filled her ears. She gripped the arm-rests, and found it hard to swallow.

They tumbled, over and over. The sensors showed the swirling water, angry streaks of foaming white amid the darkness. Then the sensors cut out, and the Proteus lost power.

Ryann closed her eyes.

There was nothing they could do. The water pummelled them from all sides. She felt collisions, and heard hideous scraping sounds—other debris smashing against them. And within the bridge, when she pushed out to the others, all she tasted was their fear, sharp and pungent.

And then they shot forward, with such force that Ryann feared she would lose consciousness. She swallowed vomit, her face cold and clammy, and her chest squeezed tight.

But she continued to analyse. She understood how they had been forced along the huge stopper at the base of the waterfall, until they had reached a weaker spot. Then, the force of the water had been released, and they had been rejected into the river.

They spun, but gently now. The water tilted them at times, and now they rolled and tilted to starboard, and came to a stop with a grinding crunch of metal on rock.

The fear from the crew settled, and relief pushed it down. She heard breath being forced from between pursed lips, and the stuttered shaking of something close to laughter.

They'd survived the Tumbler.

<*How we doing?*> Cathal sussed, wide to the whole crew.

<*Alive.*> That was from Keelin, and Ryann knew it was a flippant mask for her true emotions. But it meant she was fighting. It meant she was not giving in to the fear and panic that—if her high adrenaline signals were anything to go by—was still coursing through her. Ryann read the twitches of her hands and fingers, as if she were pressing buttons and swiping screens, and she knew Keelin

was running through checks on the Proteus. Doing what any good pilot would do after an emergency landing.

<*End of the day, that's all that matters,*> Cathal sussed. <*Okay, standard protocol. Scan and send to Ryann.*>

That calmed Tris. Cathal knew what he was doing, slipping into routine when things went awry. Known tasks gave the illusion of control, if nothing else.

The scans came to her, and Ryann stored them after giving each a brief but intense read.

<*What do we look like, Ryann?*> Cathal's voice was clearer when he sussed directly, cutting the others out.

It took her a couple of seconds to summarise each report.

<*No physical injuries.*>

<*Good. Wouldn't expect any.*>

<*Tris is struggling. He's holding it in at the moment, but he's scared.*>

<*Not good. Suggestions?*>

<*On a knife-edge. We need to be careful. Give him things to do, but make them meaningful. He's looking to Keelin a lot, and I'm not sure this is healthy for the crew as a whole.*>

<*Noted. Keelin?*>

<*Becoming too attached to the Proteus. You heard how she turned to Tris earlier? It's not like her to use sarcasm.*>

<*What do I need to watch for?*>

<*Not sure. I'll monitor.*>

<*As always. Brice?*>

Ryann paused. It wasn't like him to be this slow.

<*Brice?*> she sussed. <*You there?*>

<*Yeah.*>

<*You sent your scan?*>

<*Course.*> Then, after a pause, <*Resending now. You got it?*>

It came through, with a marker that indicated a physical push. That was strange, maybe worrying. Normally, the lattice pushed the scan her way as soon as it was completed.

<*Received. Everything okay?*>

<We've just gone over the Tumbler in a Proteus with glitching power, and we're in the middle of the biggest storm of the season so far. I'm peachy.>

He wasn't, but at least he was trying to keep his spirits up.

Ryann perused his scan before reporting to Cathal, although she was unsure how to phrase this.

<First glance, Brice's scan seems fine. But he had to push. And I couldn't reach him when we went over the fall.>

<Be specific. Dark?>

<Felt that way.>

<He turned his lattice off because he was scared?>

<Doubtful. I think it was involuntary.>

Cathal paused. *<That's not good.>*

<No.>

Ryann knew that was potential trouble.

Going dark was part of training, and some people even liked the sensation. But that was a conscious decision. When a lattice failed, it was usually during tweaking, when medics and tech teams would be on hand to reboot. A lattice fail in the field could be catastrophic. Ryann had only heard of two such incidents, and both resulted in fatalities.

<He aware he went dark?>

<Can't see how he wasn't.>

<But he's keeping it to himself.>

If Brice was going dark, that would impact the whole crew.

<I'll keep a close eye on him,> she sussed, even though that didn't feel like it would be enough. <What about you, Cathal? You okay?>

<You tell me.>

Ryann knew he was smiling. She glanced through his scan, although it told her little she didn't already know.

<Calm. Analysing. I'm sure you're planning our next move.> That was a fairly standard assessment, but his playfulness was masking worries. She needed to help him. *<Bit of an adrenaline spike earlier—probably understandable, and I'm sure it was as much to do with concern for the crew as for your own well-being.>* Ryann allowed her tone to lift; an equivalent of a wry grin.

Cathal didn't respond instantly. He shook with a silent laugh.

<You know, for a clinical tracker, you can be far too smooth at times, Miss Harris. Far too smooth.>

And there it was—his inner warmth. He wouldn't allow the rest of the crew to see it, but if Ryann could coax that from him, she knew he was at ease with himself. If she could keep the troubles of his command from clouding his thoughts, then he could lead them to safety.

Ryann smiled. Cathal was in control, and she had faith in him.

Three

When the Proteus came to rest, Brice let his fingers relax, wondering when he'd gripped the arm rests so tightly.

His neck was sore. His lattice reported mild whiplash, and it was already firing impulses to correct any damage. There was a bruise on his arm, and he had no recollection of when that happened.

Brice looked around the cabin. The light was dim, like they were on emergency power. The Proteus lay on its side, and although Keelin and Tris were still in front of Brice's seat, Ryann was now underneath him. If his restraint gave, he'd land on top of her. He doubted she'd look so calm then.

But as she analysed their scans—and Brice was annoyed he had to push his—she seemed relaxed. She even smiled at one point.

"Keelin, report." Cathal's voice was loud, but only because there were no other sounds in the cabin.

"Just completing diagnostic." She looked uncomfortable, with her hair falling away to the side of her head. "Full report logged."

"Give us a verbal summary."

"Resting on the river bed, mixture of rock and mud, so unstable." Keelin's voice was flat. "Completely submerged. Out of the main flow, roughly twenty metres from the nearest bank."

"And the Proteus?"

Keelin took a long breath before answering. "Hull holding, but the data contains anomalies. Not too sure what that means.

Power's…temperamental. Some of the data streams are elusive."

"I don't need uncertainty, Keelin."

"Sorry. This baby's hurting. It's like she doesn't want me prodding where she's injured. It's like she's curling up on herself."

It annoyed Brice when Keelin talked like the craft was sentient. The Proteus was a piece of kit, all tech. The river was more alive than this hunk of metal.

"Okay. This is what we do," Cathal said. "Keelin—keep working on the craft, see what you can do. Tris—work on the systems, focusing on contact with Haven. Ryann—check externals. Brice—cabin, manual check."

Ryann's head jerked towards Cathal. It must've been a private suss.

"And Brice."

"Cathal?"

"Keep in contact. Report anything."

"Will do." He looked around the bridge. "Once I get there."

Cathal nodded, and then his eyes glazed as he retreated into his lattice, doing whatever he did while the others worked. And the others sat almost as motionless, all working internally. He was the only one who needed to leave his seat. Typical.

And with the Proteus on its side, this wasn't going to be easy.

He grabbed the seat with his hands and tensed his body. He told his lattice to release the restraints slowly.

"You want me to move?" Ryann asked. Brice looked down at her. She had one eyebrow raised, but didn't look worried that he'd fall.

Tris shuffled in his seat, turning to watch.

The easiest thing would be to ask Ryann to move, and then he could drop. But where would be the fun in that?

Beneath her, the hull of the craft was a smooth wall. Smooth enough to walk on.

"No need," he answered. "Could do with the exercise."

His restraints parted, and he gripped his seat as he swung his legs, building momentum. And then he released.

Brice's boots hit the wall with a thud, and Keelin flinched. Probably upset that he'd scuffed her baby.

"What, no somersault?" said Tris. Brice ignored his jealousy.

The door to the cabin ran on a self-contained system, and slid back when Brice pushed the release. With the tilt of the Proteus, the opening was at head height. He grabbed the frame and jumped, balancing on the thin lip, his lattice pushing and pulling at his muscles, synchronised to keep him from tipping too far either way. He smiled, relishing the control.

It was dark, the dim glow from the bridge failing to penetrate beyond a metre or so. Brice called up night filters on his lenses, and objects glowed green. He added other filters, and the image morphed into something almost like normal. Almost, but everything had an indistinct edge, like a dream.

"Be back in a bit," he said.

"Be back when you've done a thorough check," said Cathal.

"That's what I meant."

He jumped and let the door seal behind him.

The cabin was about twice the size of the bridge. For this mission, Cathal had ordered standard config, so there was a table in the middle, and a bench along the wall that was now at his feet. The bench was locked upright, which made walking across it so much easier.

He started at the crew's quarters. He'd never liked that term, and didn't care that it was traditional. The fractional sound of it just reminded him how small each one was.

Five of them, of course, little more than pods in the wall. Five quarters—something else that annoyed Brice. Each contained storage and a mattress, giving just enough space to sleep.

Home away from home, Cathal always said. Brice was never sure if he was joking.

Cathal insisted that communal spaces were kept as clear as possible, and Keelin didn't like anything interfering with the smooth lines of her baby. But the quarters were personal. So Tris had pictures stuck to the ceiling of his—real pictures rather than projections—and Brice wondered how Data-boy could sleep with all those faces staring down at him. Keelin had a few extra cushions on her red fleece topper, and Ryann had crisp white bedding against green mottled walls that, he assumed, reminded her of the forest or something. Brice's quarters were nothing special, and although Cathal said they were a mess, Brice just thought of them as his.

Of course, Cathal stuck to standard-issue bedroll and plain walls.

Brice sealed up each of the quarters as he checked it, then moved on to the storage units and kitchen area. Everything was in its place—tools, utensils, foodstuffs, extra clothing. And their pathetic array of weapons.

Brice loved firearm training, and he'd looked forward to using those weapons in the field. But the company didn't allow that. Kaiahive were setting up outposts, not invading enemy territory. The area had been scanned by drones, and there was no need for lethal weapons. Even the warths were not dangerous if left to themselves.

And so, for the sake of the company's image, the crews had no firepower. Everyone held a lash, true, but these only sent out a short burst of energy. Hit a warth with one, and if you got it right, you might knock the beast over. And, as the company said, that should give you enough time to get the hell out of there.

So their weapons were next to useless.

Of course, the company allowed them to carry knives. But they were tools, not weapons. They were for cutting through undergrowth, not for hacking at living things.

He pushed through the door into the heads, and nothing was amiss—two shower cubicles, toilet, couple of sinks. The mirrored storage was sealed and, when he opened it, nothing moved. Another of Cathal's demands—always use webbing. Just in case.

<No problems so far,> he sussed. Of course there weren't. This task was pointless, something that had to be done to tick a box in Cathal's mental check-list. As usual, Brice got the donkey-work.

And why? Because he was green. To Cathal, he'd always be the newbie, and he'd never be good enough.

Brice pulled out of the heads, shutting the slightly lemony, slightly medical smell behind him. Just the hatches left to check.

There were two of them, the main hatch to port (now over Brice's head), and the smaller reserve hatch in the topside. As far as Brice could tell, that was one of the few times the company actually put major money into a safety feature. Of course, they had little choice after that crew had been trapped in the burning Proteus. They talked of learning lessons, and of ensuring those lives had not been lost in vain, but it was clear what they were doing—limiting damages. As usual, they were looking after their own backs.

But they did install reserve hatches in all craft after that.

Brice had only ever used one in training, crawling through the hatch as dense smoke filled the craft, his lattice warning him of danger that he knew was only a simulation programmed by the trainers. But he'd still felt the adrenaline rush.

The door was circular, with a number pad in the middle. He keyed in the release code, not wishing to use the emergency override. That would trigger all kinds of signals, and probably annoy the hell out of Keelin. And then Cathal would have a go at him for upsetting his crew, like he wasn't supposed to even be there.

The door hissed and dropped back, swinging on heavy hinges. The movement was quicker than Brice expected, and he stumbled out of the way, putting a hand out to steady himself but falling anyway. The impact jarred him, and for a moment his lenses flashed, and a sharp bolt of pain surged through his head.

He swore under his breath and brought a hand up to his temple, where he'd struck the wall. It felt tender, and he winced as his fingers probed. Shaking his head to clear the grogginess, he punched the hatch door. Stupid, pointless job! There was nothing to find. Any problems would show up on sensors, even with the Proteus on emergency power. This was nothing more than a way to get Brice out of the way, to keep him occupied. What else was he good for?

But he'd see this through. Just the hatches to check, then he'd go back up front and give his report. Maybe make a spreadsheet, like Tris would, building a simple task into something important, making out it was life-and-death.

If Tris was so good at his job, why hadn't he contacted Haven yet? Why were they stuck here?

Brice looked into the hatch. It was dim; green and murky. That was the filters on his lenses, he told himself. But the lines were indistinct. Usually, these settings gave him a crisper image.

Maybe that was because of the hatch being a cylinder. Maybe the curves distorted the filters somehow.

But when he looked back into the cabin, the murkiness remained. It was nothing he could put his finger on, just a general…haziness. Like he was looking through a semi-transparent film, or like he was underwater.

He almost laughed at that thought, remembering exactly where the Proteus lay.

Maybe it was a lens glitch, or something in the stale air from the hatch. It was nothing to worry about.

<Just the main hatch to check. No problems so far.> But he'd take his time. Go back too soon, and Cathal would find some other crap for him to do, like cleaning the heads.

The main hatch was large enough for three to walk through at a time. It had to be, in case they needed to exit at speed. That was the phrase used in training—not 'make an emergency exit', or 'get the hell out of there', but 'exit at speed'.

With the angle of the Proteus, the hatch was way above Brice. He climbed onto the side of the table, balancing carefully as he reached up. He ran a hand round the outer edge of the door, where it sat smoothly against the inner hull of the craft, cool beneath his fingers.

But there was one patch, to his left, that felt a few degrees cooler than the rest. Brice let his hand linger, and he focused on the tilt of the craft. The Proteus lay not only on its side, but also facing ever so slightly nose-up. That mean the cooler patch was to the aft of the door. Brice knew that should be important.

He connected with the door controls and gave it the instruction to open. It slid to one side, opening up the hatch chamber.

Brice swallowed. They were in trouble.

On instinct he pulled up more filters, but he didn't need to do that in order to see the darker patch. An ominous deep green ran from the outer door to where his hand still rested on that cooler patch.

And it did run. It flowed towards his hand.

Brice screamed for his lattice to seal the hatch, and it slid shut with a hiss. He took a breath, calming himself, and he wavered for a moment on the edge of the table, his hand still on the cooler patch.

It was larger now, and he could feel the moisture.

His mouth was dry.

Brice opened up his lattice to the rest of the crew, and sussed.

<We've got a breach.>

FOUR

Brice got no response. He tried telling himself the dampness beneath his hand was just sweat, but he'd never been good at lying to himself.

He closed his eyes, the misty green after-image in his lenses fading to a washed-out black.

<*Getting more power now. Enough to dive deeper.*> It was Keelin. She sounded fraught.

<*I'm getting it too. Directing some juice to seeker routines, see if we can throw something far enough.*> That was Tris, although the words made little sense to Brice. He guessed it was to do with calling Haven.

<*Don't grab it all. First priority's security. I want to make sure this baby's okay.*>

Brice swore under his breath, and shouted back at her. <*We're not okay. We've got a breach!*>

He connected to the sensors within the hatch. At first they slipped from his grip, but he focused and held them, zooming into the monochrome image. The water—and he couldn't pretend it was anything else now—flowed with mercurial slivers from outer to inner hatch. And where it started there was a kink in the metal. It was the slightest of misalignments, but it was enough.

<*Brice. Anything to report?*>

What the hell?

<Already reported, Cathal. We're breached.>

What was the point of sending him back here and then ignoring what he said?

<Getting something,> Keelin sussed. *<Raised moisture levels, rear of the craft. Focusing in now.>*

Brice felt a chill run through him. And something dropped onto his head.

He looked up, moving his hand across to the edge of the inner hatch. Liquid ran towards his finger, pooling until it could no longer support its own weight, and then it fell, landing on his cheek like an icy pin-prick.

<Power's pulling back, Keelin. I can't raise anything. You doing that?>

<More important things to do, Tris. Back me up, will you?>

<Where we going?>

<Sub-route beta nine. Track fifteen to nineteen. I've got the rest. Patch any findings to core monitoring.>

The words flowed through Brice, but there was more, in the background, from two other voices.

<Thoughts, Ryann?>

<Already reaching out beyond the river. Warths in this area, but shouldn't be a problem.>

<Safe areas?>

<Depends on your definition. A hold-out ninety minutes away, maybe more with current conditions. Have a look.>

Images burst into Brice's mind, a series of maps and stills that blurred into a meaningless grey.

<Chances if we have to abandon?> Cathal asked.

<Gut reaction, pretty high.>

He shouldn't be hearing this. Although he was receiving wide, this conversation was private. He shouldn't be able to eavesdrop.

<The family?>

<Holding up, but I have my concerns.>

<About?>

<Brice.>

Brice held himself rigid, not sure if he wanted to hear this.

<*Give me specifics.*>

<*It's that distance I told you of. Dark, but not dark.*>

<*You're not making much sense.*>

<*I know. It worries me. He could go either way.*>

What did that mean?

<*And yourself, Ryann?*>

<*Concerned. I don't want us to be another disappearance.*>

<*Understood.*>

There was a lull, and then Ryann came back.

<*And I don't want you going melancholy on us, Cathal.*>

<*Not the time or place.*>

<*Exactly. Leave that for later.*>

That meant absolutely nothing to Brice.

Another drop of water landed on his forehead.

<*We're taking in water!*> he yelled. <*Main hatch. Keelin, you reading this?*>

There was no response. He heard more technobabble between Keelin and Tris, like they were talking in another language. There was something about hull integrity, and they both sounded worried.

Brice considered sussing again, but what was the point? They couldn't hear him. It was like he existed in his own bubble back here.

That must be it. With the Proteus running on emergency power, and all its systems playing up, there must be interference. The craft itself was blocking his messages.

Brice returned to the bridge, trying to ignore the obvious—if they couldn't hear him, how could he hear them?

"Welcome back, Brice. Pleasant break?"

Brice kept his voice level, countering the sarcasm. "We've got a breach."

That got their attention. Keelin spun in her chair, and Cathal looked round with one eye cocked. Even Tris turned.

"Main hatch. Possibly damage to the outer door, and water's pooling. It's starting to seep through the inner door."

Keelin's eyes glazed over for a second. "Of course," she said to herself, and her shoulders sagged.

"How serious?" Cathal turned to his pilot.

"Getting readings. Don't want to pull power from core functions."

"We're not going to have those core functions if it's flooded," Brice said.

"Bit of water won't hurt it," said Tris, and Brice caught his sneer.

"Maybe. How long can you hold your breath?"

<Behave. You're professionals.> This came from Ryann, and Brice didn't know if it was wide, or targeted just to himself and Tris. But he nodded. She was right. This wasn't the time for the tech-monkey to get all superior.

"Keelin?" Cathal asked.

"Data now in. Situation serious, but not dire. The flow is increasing, and the breach widening. At current rates, the hatch will fill in twenty minutes, and increased pressure will widen the gap in the inner door. Rough estimate, forty to fifty minutes before we're swimming."

"So under an hour of air left."

"Going on current data, yes."

"And power? That going to get back up any time soon?"

Brice saw Keelin hesitate, and turn to Tris, who shrugged.

"Seems unlikely."

Brice took in a breath and held it before releasing. He felt the twin thuds of his heartbeat, and he suppressed the release of adrenaline. He didn't need that yet.

Cathal brought a hand up to his chin with the sandpaper rustle of skin over bristles.

"Keelin, open prediction—what can we expect from the Proteus?"

Keelin shook her head. "I've never seen her like this. She needs help, more than I can give her. Without that, she'll slip into deep sleep. Maybe a few hours, maybe a couple of minutes."

"I thought these things were tough?" Brice fought to control his anger. "Aren't they supposed to be able to withstand just about anything? What about all that crap about how they're tested in lava and zero atmospheres, and flown at mountainsides to make sure they survive? A tumble down a waterfall should be nothing."

He felt Ryann's eyes on him, but he kept his own on Keelin. Unfair, he knew, but he needed a focus. And she met his gaze with coldness.

"It should be. But the systems are electrical at core. A lightning strike can play havoc with that."

"And they didn't think to protect against that?"

"They did! When this baby came off the production line, she was perfect. But she's old. You know how it goes. You know how the company cuts corners."

"So we're screwed because some bean counter didn't want to spend too much?"

"What, you think you're worth anything to Kaiahive?" She spat out the company's name.

"That's enough!" Ryann held a hand out, a thin barrier between Brice and Keelin. It was enough to make him take a step back.

"That's life," Cathal said. "Get used to it. They make the decisions, we cope with the fall-out. That's what they pay us for." He looked from Brice to Keelin and back again. "Or are you only doing this for the thrill of it?"

Brice didn't need to answer. Nor did Keelin. Cathal continued.

"Situation's this. Lightning screwed up our Proteus, and we're taking on water. Storm's worsening, and it's already dark enough for night. We need to exit, and we need to be prepared. Ryann, take Brice and sort out kit. Tris, you work with Keelin."

Tris nodded, and swallowed.

"Tell me," Cathal said. "Tell me what we need to do."

Brice knew. They all did. It was part of the training, but nobody expected to have to use it for real.

Tris avoided everyone's eyes as he spoke. "We need to flood the Proteus."

FIVE

Ryann eased herself from her chair, joining Brice on the wall.

She could tell he was scared. He wouldn't admit that, even to himself, but the signs were there—dilated pupils, the flickering movements of his face, the way his fingers twitched when he talked. And, of course, there was his anger. She felt it rolling off him, but it was undirected. He was searching for a reason, for something to be angry at. And that was unhealthy.

<*Keep me informed,*> Cathal sussed.

<*Will do.*>

She met Brice's eyes and tilted her head to the open door. He nodded and climbed smoothly. Of course he did. Physicality was his speciality. If she could keep him moving, he'd stay calm.

In the cabin, she reached up to seal the door, but Brice put his own hand in the way, cupping the sensor without triggering it.

"Can we leave the door open?" he said. "I think it was stopping communication before. Interference or something."

"Of course." She pulled her own hand back. The door might muffle sound, but it was not a barrier to communication. Brice looked away, and Ryann sensed there was more he wanted to say.

She wouldn't push him. She'd give him time to collect his thoughts. She'd give him a nudge later.

"Let's get started," she said, moving to the storage units. "Overnight kit."

He raised his eyebrows at that.

"Just a precaution. But seal everything tight."

"Watertight."

"Exactly. You ready for this?" Keeping things vague let his mind go where it needed.

"Course. Just like training, right?"

Brice opened a unit and pulled out a pack without looking. *Exactly* like training, Ryann thought. Brice emptied the contents, checking. She imagined that, like her, he ran through a list in his mind —micro-rope, emergency aid kit, sleepsac, water bottle, and so on.

It was honest work, and it diverted his mind. Now might be a good time to delve into the things that were troubling her.

"You mentioned interference?" She pulled out a second pack, mirroring Brice's actions.

He shrugged. "I sussed about the breach, but got no response. I could hear you — all of you — but it was like you couldn't hear me."

He was tightening straps on the pack, from bottom to top. Ryann did the same, without consciously glancing at either her pack or his.

"Can you hear them now?" she asked.

Brice nodded.

"Anything interesting?" She needed to know he wasn't bluffing.

He shrugged. "Wouldn't call it interesting. Keelin and Tris are talking through the procedure for flooding the Proteus, and Cathal is interrupting."

Interrupting. That was an interesting choice of word. Listening in herself, Ryann knew he was guiding them, using questions to force them to consider other factors. Interrupting suggested interference, not assistance.

She'd have to monitor Brice's attitude towards Cathal.

<*Shouldn't be long with the packs,*> she sussed, sending wide. "You catch that?" she asked Brice.

"Loud and clear." He put one pack aside and moved on to the next. Ryann did the same.

Then she thought of his pause earlier, and focused on Cathal alone. <*The kids behaving up there?*>

<*Playing nicely.*> Cathal kept his response tight.

"Hear anything else?" she asked Brice, keeping her voice nonchalant.

His brow furrowed, and his throat bobbed. "Just Keelin going on about pressure. Think that's what it is." He shrugged. "Never was good at that stuff. But she doesn't sound bothered, so that's a good sign, right?"

Ryann smiled. "Must be."

And he'd given too much away. The levity in his voice was forced. He'd hesitated a fraction too long, and she'd noticed his body twitch. And that meant…

She wasn't sure what it meant. She needed more data.

"Ask Cathal something, Brice. Anything at all."

He shrugged again, still tugging at webbing on the pack, feigning apathy. His brow furrowed. He glanced at her, and when she didn't respond—when she forced her expression to remain passive—he looked away, moving on to the last pack. Ryann grabbed the other four, placing them by the open door.

"Suspected as much," she said, quietly, as if talking to herself. When he turned, she paused, with one eyebrow raised, as if to say 'what?' He didn't speak, and before his slightly confused expression dissolved into resentment—as it surely must if he believed her to be holding out on him—she spoke, louder. "Tell me, what were you doing when the lightning struck?"

His hands stopped moving over the pack, and his eyes looked up. He pulled his lower lip between his teeth, biting gently. Ryann wondered if he was conscious that he always did that when he was deep in thought.

"I was riding the hull."

And that meant his lattice was joined to the external of the Proteus when the lightning struck.

"That makes sense," she said, giving him something to hold on to. "A big enough charge could disrupt a lattice, although there's normally protection."

"You saying the lightning fried my lattice?"

That was putting it crudely, but it would suffice. She nodded. “It’ll need checking out, of course. I could run a quick diagnostic?” She extended her hand. Brice looked at it, hesitating. That was understandable. If she were in his position, she’d be uncomfortable about what might be uncovered, too.

And then water splashed onto her hand, the droplet exploding in a green glow. She looked up, to the hatchway, and to the dark patch around the seal. Another drop of water peeled off and fell.

<*Those packs ready?*> Cathal’s voice cut through her thoughts, pushing aside the background chatter from Keelin and Tris.

She looked down at the five bundles. <*They are,*> she sussed.

<*Might want to bring them through here. Things are about to get very wet.*>

Six

Brice grabbed three of the packs, Ryann the other two. When she nodded, he made his way back through the door. But not before he saw how the drips were now a continual flow of water.

In the bridge, everyone was out of their seats, standing on the wall. They grabbed their packs and shouldered them. Nobody spoke, or—as far as Brice could tell—even looked at one another. The whole scene felt like a training session, but one that shouldn't be happening.

He adjusted the straps on his own pack, pulling it firmly against his back. He bounced and rolled his shoulders, checking for any friction. There was none.

And that felt comforting. The pack was a part of him, just like his jacket and his boots. He mentally ran through an inventory of everything he carried, either on his back or in pockets, and each item appeared as a picture in his mind.

He didn't know if that was in his own mind or through his lattice. Ryann's words hovered over everything, spreading possible implications like cracks across glass. He couldn't trust his lattice any more. His muscles would need to function on their own, with no back-up. His senses would be dulled. When adrenaline flowed—like it was doing so now—it would be uncontrolled.

Brice used to enjoy training dark. But this was no longer training.

Splashing water echoed form the cabin, like someone pouring a never-ending drink. Brice looked into the gloom, and wondered why he couldn't see a puddle, until he realised the whole wall shimmered and rippled.

The water rose, and broke through into the bridge, tumbling around the door in its own little waterfall. Nothing as impressive as the Tumbler, but it hypnotised Brice, how the water cascaded down, individual drops consumed by the whole, all working together like some vast living organism. The amorphous beast stretched out, surrounding the crew. The water reached Brice's ankles, then crept over the top of his boots.

It was cold, but he sensed the temperature rather than feeling it, and he wondered if his lattice was retaining body heat, or if adrenaline was numbing him to any pain. The effect was the same either way, so maybe it didn't matter. He twisted his legs, moving the slight pressure from his calves to his shins and back, playing with the water. It was something to do while he waited.

The water rose, creeping over his skin like icy fingers, his trousers and then jacket wicking the moisture up even higher. His skin pulled tight in anticipation, and he gasped as the coldness hit his chest. As it reached his chin, he tilted his head back and his feet lifted from the ground.

Or, rather, from the wall. Brice kicked upwards, then pedalled his feet, keeping himself afloat.

The water was murky. He could no longer see his legs, and when he dipped a hand beneath the surface it disappeared from view. There were other shapes, blobs that would be the crew's bodies, but nothing was defined.

Run-off. That was the technical term, wasn't it? With the storm, loads of soil and whatever else was being flushed into the river, and this was all being thrown over the Tumbler. The plunge pool would be churning everything up, and now that water had almost filled the Proteus. Water that was more than just a liquid.

He didn't want to think about what else it contained.

<How's the hatch, Keelin?> Cathal asked.

<Ready for release once we're full.>

Brice looked around bridge, at least what was still above the surface. The wall above was closer now. Of the two forward seats, one was already submerged. Tris', Brice noted, and that pleased him. But the water only took a few seconds to reach Keelin's seat. Soon, only a small air pocket would remain.

He took a long breath, stretching then squeezing his lungs, pushing them to their limit. He didn't know how long he'd be under for. The short swim to the hatch wasn't a problem, but Brice had no idea what to expect after that. The flow might be strong enough to carry him further downstream. There might be fallen trees to negotiate. The Proteus might be deeper than they knew.

Too many possibilities.

Something collided with Brice's head, and he moved to one side, away from his own chair. The door to the cabin was now underwater, and only the air pocket remained.

<Releasing hatch.>

An influx of cold water swirled round his body, and he pulled in breath with a shudder. He felt silt against his skin.

Cathal moved to one side of the door. "Okay, time to move. Ryann on point, followed by Keelin, Tris, Brice. I'll bring up the rear." He grinned, water droplets shaking from his stubble. "Let's go swim."

Ryann took a breath, then dropped beneath the surface, becoming nothing more than a vague shape that passed through the door into the darkness beyond.

Keelin followed, then Tris. Data-monkey floundered for a moment, trying something like a surface dive, one foot coming up to bang loudly on the wall. Brice held his laugh in, not wanting to swallow any of the water.

When Cathal nodded, Brice brought his hands up and let the weight of his boots and pack pull him down. At the last moment he filled his lungs and sealed his mouth.

Even with lenses, it was hard to see beneath the surface. The water was gritty, and tasted foul. He pulled himself into the cabin, grabbing the table and then pushing upwards, through the hatch.

Then he was in the river, and the water was colder than he expected. The flow pulled at him, but he kicked against it, simultaneously pulling the water with cupped hands. The motion of swimming in full kit felt strangely comforting.

It took him a moment to realise he'd broken the surface, because the water didn't stop. It simply changed from a constant swirl to the heavy rapid-fire downpour of the rain.

Shapes slid through the water, towards the bank with the wall of trees. One splashed more than the other two. Only a fool like Tris would try an overarm stroke.

Brice kicked, bringing his arms round in the water, and followed. A few strokes, no more than about ten, and his hands found branches, and he pulled himself through the detritus thrown to the edge of the river. Some of it came away in his hands, some of it held him. He pushed with his legs, and occasionally his feet found purchase. A couple of times they sunk into what he hoped was only mud, and his legs strained as he freed them. But he never stopped. Hand over hand, now under a branch, now half-out of the water, he worked his way to the bank.

And then he was out, grabbing a solid tree to stand up. He coughed, and thought he'd gag. The river taste coated his tongue, and he tilted his head back, letting the rain run down the back of his throat.

Ryann, Keelin and Tris stood a short way off, looking out across the river, and Brice followed their gaze. He could just about make out the far bank through the downpour, the dark trees merging with the black clouds that hung heavy. The surface of the river itself was a rolling beast, wide and dangerous. As he watched, a shape span past, too big to be a simple branch. The river threw the small tree around like it was nothing.

Just as it had done with the Proteus.

Cathal stood by his side. Brice hadn't seen him climb out.

<Okay, we need to move. Keep to silent communication, and follow Ryann. We'll make for the cliff.>

<Not making for shelter?> sussed Keelin.

<We're close enough to the cliff, we might as well do a little recon. Full protocol, so get recording.>

<How far's the nearest hold-out?> The question came from Tris, but it was what Brice was thinking, too.

<Ryann, let them know.>

<These conditions, direct route, ninety minutes plus.>

<So we go via the cliff, add about forty-five minutes, an hour tops. I know it's not what you want, but it's called making the best of a bad situation.> Brice could imagine Cathal grinning. *<It's not like the rain's going to make us any wetter.>*

Ryann walked into the forest. Brice took one last look over the river. He could not see any sign of the Proteus. The river had claimed it.

Then he turned, and followed the others into the trees.

SEVEN

<*Ryann, tell me how we're doing.*>

<*Keelin's withdrawing, Tris is holding up so far. Brice is...Brice.*> That wasn't anywhere near an adequate description, and she knew it. <*And you're hiding, as usual.*>

<*It's called doing the job. What about you?*>

<*I'm fine.*> Although, in truth, Ryann hadn't given her own feelings much thought. Like Cathal, she had a job to do. The crew were her priority, and now she had to lead them safely through the forest. She had no time for emotions.

<*You always are.*> There was a hint of a rebuke in Cathal's words, but she'd let that pass. <*How's the path?*>

<*Warth territory,*> she answered, knowing just what he needed to hear. <*Picking up signals of cubs, so there's a nest nearby. Many old trails, but a couple of fresh ones. This weather's not helping analysis.*>

<*Nothing we haven't seen before.*>

That was almost encouragement, although she couldn't decipher if he was referring to the weather or the warths.

The forest was rich with trails, crossing through the undergrowth. One tasted of old age, with the flavour of decay waiting to pounce, a taste that Ryann had learnt to associate with death. That wasn't always a bad thing, though, and she reminded herself that all things died. She could picture the old warth, curling up one last time, its fur tinged with grey where the pelt grew thin and wiry. Ryann could imagine it closing its eyes and taking a final breath.

Even beasts deserved their peace.

But there were younger trails too, of warths in their prime. And the cubs. Ryann spotted abandoned nests against thick tree trunks, the gathered branches now discarded in lazy heaps.

She guided them along the most sensible path, keeping clear of the denser undergrowth. This felt like an abandoned warth track, from the way the creepers spread across the ground. She stored details of the plant life as a matter of course—the thick, waxy leaves of the garithus, the almond-scented tendrils of corrack-grass—but only took active interest when the data told her something. Like the patches of Fingol's lichen that appeared on trees to their right. That told her those tree-roots did not run as deep, and that in turn spoke of rockier soil.

Ryann guided the crew, using the lichen to aim for the cliff. The warth-trails would be thinner there. They were creatures of the forest, and although they were adept at climbing trees, their claws didn't grip to rock.

The trees stopped some five metres back, leaving an uneven path of mud, moss and rock. Scattered branches reached up to brush the cliff, and rain fell in a fine, penetrating drizzle. Water coated the rock, too, and she brushed it with her hand, even though it was not a living thing, and so would always be cold to her. Yet she analysed, following cracks and bulges, and spotting what might be an opening to a cave about twenty metres up.

The top of the cliff was beyond her view, and was of no concern to Ryann. She focused on the trees, where a few warth trails still ran.

Cathal sussed to the others, using tight communication but letting her receive. That gave her distance to analyse the communication. Tris' confidence was only skin-deep, but Cathal focused him on analysing data, keeping him occupied. Keelin had sealed the Proteus as far as she could, but was still hurting. Her craft was in pain, and there was nothing she could do about it.

Ryann could understand that. She remembered when her father had sick livestock on the farm. He'd say she was too sentimental, and she knew that keeping them alive only increased their suffering. But it still pained her when he had to put them down.

The Proteus was sick. When—she refused to use the word 'if'—the craft returned to Haven, the damage might be too severe.

<*You doing okay, Brice?*> Ryann noted how Cathal used the lad's name. That was good. <*Swim not too bad?*> Again, a suitable choice of words. That would appeal to Brice's confidence in his abilities.

She pushed for Brice's lattice, but a movement distracted her, and she focused into the trees. Something shifted, off to her left, about fifty metres back.

<*Ryann, you catch Brice's response?*>

<*Not now. Busy.*> She didn't want to appear brusque, but he'd understand.

She scanned the area around the movement. A branch hung loose, a fresh rip, and she could just make out the pale flesh from inside the tree.

Warths only caused damage like that when they were agitated.

The deep rumble of thunder rolled over her. The flash of lightning was filtered by the tree cover, and that gave enough light for Ryann to see the beast clearly.

It crouched by a tree, half-hidden, one paw raised, claws pressing into a branch. The fur on its flank gently rose and fell as it breathed, but otherwise it was motionless. The warth's nostrils flared, the red interior visible for a moment. Ryann scanned down to its chest, and the nipples hidden beneath the fur. The surrounding tissue was swollen, a sign that this warth was lactate-ready.

A new mother. She'd be protective of her cubs, and there was a strong possibility that she'd have a mate.

And now she caught his trail. Further off, but moving in. The male was smaller than the female, but that didn't make it any less of a threat.

Ryann raised a hand, bringing the crew to a halt. She crouched, peering into the trees, and knew the crew followed her actions. She could smell their nerves.

The female warth eased round a tree, and took a slow step closer. The male copied her movements, but from the opposite direction. Ryann followed their trajectories, and saw how they converged on the crew.

<*We've got company,*> she sussed.

EIGHT

Brice had only even seen warths from a distance. Training didn't count. The simulations couldn't rip your limbs from your body and tear out your insides before you fell to the ground, or plough into you so hard that your bones shattered.

He lowered into a crouch, just like Ryann, and peered through the trees. The wind and rain kept everything in motion. He might be looking straight at a warth and not even know it.

<*Two of them. Sending info.*>

Brice waited. Ryann was good at this. She'd capture images from her lenses, and annotate them before passing them on to the crew. It would be like looking at one of those picture-within-a-picture things, where at first you see nothing, no matter how hard you stare, but once you uncover the hidden object, you can't unsee it.

But no images came. He saw nothing beyond the vision through his own eyes, filtered through his lenses.

<*You sent it yet?*> he asked. But he was drowned out by the voices of the others, coming so fast he couldn't distinguish who sussed what.

<*Two of them? Thought they were loners.*>

<*You forgetting basic training, Tris? Not near a nest.*>

<*I can see the one ahead now. Big bugger. Biggest I've seen.*>

<*Like you've seen so many.*>

<*How many have you seen, Keelin? And I don't mean from the Proteus.*>

<*Okay. Ryann, Keelin—you track the one coming along the cliff path. Brice, Tris—keep watching the one ahead.*>

<*They're not moving. Neither of them.*>

<*That's good, right?*>

<*Alive, watching us, and not moving. That's not good.*>

<*Brice, you okay?*>

He nodded in response to Ryann, and scanned the forest. He'd caught sight of one now, the beast Cathal wanted him and Tris to track. A part of the undergrowth wasn't moving, and it slowly took on the form of a body. It was big, even crouched down like that. He didn't want to imagine what it was like raised on its hind legs.

It was watching them. He could tell by the way it shifted its head, and the way its nose twitched. He could just about make out two eyes, like thin slits that reflected what little light there was.

Brice turned his head, trying to catch sight of the second warth, the one Cathal had said was coming along the cliff path. Did that mean it was moving their way? If that was the case, shouldn't they be retreating? That was the standard procedure—stop, and if the warth came closer, retreat. Make no sudden movements, and do nothing to appear threatening. They wouldn't attack unless provoked. They were harmless until they believed they were in danger. Or their cubs were at risk.

Ryann had mentioned a nest.

The beast in the trees made a snuffling noise, and Brice saw its lips part, revealing grey teeth. Brice gulped. He knew they were mainly herbivores, but that didn't calm him. They would eat meat when pushed, or when there was no other option, and their jaws were powerful enough to tear through skin and muscle as easily as taking a bite from a piece of fruit.

Brice wondered if flesh tasted as sweet.

<*Our friend by the cliff is getting closer,*> Ryann sussed. <*Think we might have to retreat.*>

<*Think?*> Cathal's voice was sharp.

<*Not a threat yet.*>

<*How fast can those things run again?*> Sounded like Tris was close to panic.

<*Just keep calm. The one in the forest up to much?*>

<*Watching us. Hasn't moved yet. Looks kind of bored.*> At least Tris was looking where he should have been.

Brice glanced back, to the path they'd walked in on. Many of the plants had sprung back into place, but he could still make out their route where they'd broken some. He doubted that was Ryann, even though she'd been first through. Probably Tris, being heavy-handed.

And something caught his eye. A shape, just behind a couple of low-hanging branches. Something big.

But they never travelled in threes. On their own, or in pairs near a nest. Put a third warth in the mix, and they'd fight amongst themselves.

Yet what else could it be?

<*Think we've got a third joining the party. Back the way we came.*>

Brice focused. The fur was lighter, almost silver. Did that mean it was older, or younger? Maybe it wasn't important. And maybe the way it opened its jaws and stretched its face was a sign of boredom, or some kind of exercise. Maybe it was in pain, a thorn stuck in its paw or something.

And maybe it was preparing to attack.

Brice moved a hand to his hip and flicked open the catch on his holster. He knew a lash would do little to stop a warth in full run, but it might do enough. It might be sufficient to give him time to escape.

<*We can't go back.*> As Cathal sussed, Brice felt relief. At least someone was listening. <*We go up.*>

<*Up? Thought they climbed.*>

<*When we're home, Tris, I'm going to force-feed you everything we have on warths, just so I don't have to listen to your kindergarten crap again. They climb trees. They don't like rock.*>

<*That true, Ryann?*>

Brice rolled his eyes, but a part of him was worried. If Tris was forgetting stuff in his panic, what would he do if those things did attack? He'd be a bloody liability.

<*As far as we know. Cathal, what's your plan?*> Brice thought he detected an edge of worry in Ryann's voice. That wasn't good.

<*Ledge about twenty metres up, easy climb. Sending what I can see. Keep your eyes on those shaggies.*>

Brice moved back until he was against the rock. He twitched his fingers, wondering how the rain would affect the holds. But if Cathal said it looked easy, Brice would have no problems. He didn't know about the others, though. He hadn't seen them climb.

Not in the rain. And never with three angry warths at their heels.

Brice looked back to the third warth. It was slinking through the foliage, keeping low to the ground, like it was trying to stay hidden. But it was unmistakable, as were its intentions. Its gaze never once wavered from where Brice and the others stood.

He slid the lash from the holster and curled his fingers round the grip. He brought his thumb up and placed it on the control panel, calling up full power, high intensity. Anything less would be little more than a light slap. He needed a heavy punch.

The crosshairs in Brice's lenses tunnelled as he brought them together on the target, zooming in on those beady eyes and that glistening nose. He lowered his aim, to the yellow teeth, and the mottled pink of the weaker mouth tissue

Brice locked on to the target. Even if he moved the lash now, his lattice would compensate. There was no way he could miss.

Ryann urged caution, and Cathal told them to hold firm. They would wait for the first move. While the warths remained stationary, there was no danger.

<*But what about the third one?*> he sussed.

<*Get ready to climb,*> Cathal's voice was strangely distant. <*You all see routes up?*>

Brice didn't turn. He knew how to climb. He could work out a route on the fly, no problem.

The warth in his sights was smaller than the other two, but muscles rippled beneath the fur on its haunches. And now, Brice saw that it was not silvery, but was covered in mud, like it had been wallowing in a pool of the stuff.

Did warths do that?

It rocked back on its haunches, the sides of its mouth twitching. Through the constant dripping and the roll of thunder, Brice heard a guttural growl vibrate from the beast's throat. He saw the head lower as a flash of lightning lit the sky.

Brice didn't have time to shout a warning as the warth charged.

NINE

Brice squeezed the trigger and the crosshairs glowed brilliant red. The air shimmered as the burst of energy flew. For a moment he could no longer see the beast, or its open jaws. He felt his arm twitch as his lattice compensated for kick-back.

The blast hit the warth mid-jump.

The beast landed awkwardly, thrown off course but still upright. And this time the roar was loud enough to fill the forest.

<*Up. Now!*> Cathal slapped at Brice's outstretched arm, hard enough that he almost dropped his lash.

<*They're coming.*> Ryann sounded calm, but when Brice turned to her, she was already on the cliff face, and behind her a warth raced through the undergrowth.

Tris and Keelin were already climbing, as was Cathal. Brice holstered his lash, turned, and grabbed the rock. Branches cracked behind him, and he didn't know how close they were.

He pushed off with one foot, reaching up with his hands, finding one hold, then another. Cathal was right—it wasn't a hard climb. Brice moved fast. But those beasts were big. He needed height.

If they stretched up, how high could they reach? Four metres, five?

He pushed on, not sure if the roar in his ears was from the storm, the warths, or his own heart and the blood it sent round his body. He felt the warmth of muscles working, and the adrenaline rush of action.

And he was out of the danger zone now, too high for the beasts to reach. He stopped, leaning back from a vertical crack, and looked around.

The others were above him. Even Tris. Data-dork climbed just how Brice expected—thugging his way up, with no finesse or control. Keelin, on the other hand, moved with quiet efficiency, and from the way her head constantly moved, Brice knew she was constantly re-evaluating her route. Not like Tris, grabbing from one hold to the next.

Ryann and Cathal flanked them, climbing steadily. Brice knew he should be level with them, not lagging behind. But he'd give them a bit of distance, then catch up. Maybe even overtake. Show them what climbing was all about.

There was a crash from below. Brice looked down. A black shape blurred beneath him, and he felt a second crash as the warth slammed into the cliff, one limb outstretched, razor-sharp claws scraping at the rock. And further back, he saw movement from the trees. No—of the trees. One of them shook violently.

But warths didn't climb rock. They were no longer a threat.

Brice carried on climbing, closing the distance from the others. He reached into a crack, leaning away, bringing his feet up high. The next hold, one lunge away, was bomb-proof.

His boot slipped.

His knee slammed into the rock, sending a jolt of pain through his leg. His fingers started to slide. They felt hot and tight.

Brice balled his free hand into a fist and thrust it forward, jamming it into the crack. He clenched it tighter, and the rock grated against his skin.

But it held. Even when his other boot slid from the rock, his fist held.

He took a breath, heard a comment from someone, maybe Cathal, but he shut his eyes and ignored it. He took a second breath, holding it in as he scanned his body. The pain in his knee was fading fast, but his arm was pumped, the muscle too hard. And he realised his only point of contact with the rock was that fist.

Brice scrambled with his feet, and they found ledges. He swung his free arm, his fingers curling round the edge of the crack again. He transferred his weight to this hand and relaxed his fist. The skin was moist and sticky, his knuckles burning.

There was a drawn-out snap from below, cutting sharply through the drumming in Brice's ears. The tree that had been shaking started to topple, falling towards the cliff. At the base of the trunk, one of the warths leaned against it, pushing hard.

They didn't climb rock, but they climbed trees.

The tree crunched into the cliff, smaller branches crumpling under its weight, and it was close enough that Brice felt a rush of air. And then the warth grabbed the trunk and started to climb.

The tree ended above Brice, almost at the ledge. The spindly branches at the edge brushed against him.

Brice pushed the pain from his mind, and he climbed. Water cascaded down the rock. His hands moved over and over in the crack. His boots edged wherever they could.

The tree against the rock shook, and Brice heard it creak as the warth climbed.

The others were calling, but he wasn't sure if it was through his lattice or his ears. They were standing on the ledge, looking down. Even Tris.

A flash of lightning lit the sky. The ledge was just above the top of the tree. A few metres, that was all.

Could a warth make that leap?

The crew drew their lashes. Brice pushed himself on. Hand over hand, one move at a time. Arm then leg, arm then leg. Just like a ladder. Just like a walk.

Cathal barked instructions, something about a weak spot.

Brice didn't see the blur from the lashes, but he saw the tree shudder where the bolts of energy struck it. Cathal gave another yell, and they fired again.

And the tree started to move.

A warth growled, the sound rolling around Brice and making his skin tighten.

Cathal gave another signal, barked something about hurrying up, and this time Brice looked up in time to see the air blur.

There was a sharp crack. The tree shifted, and Brice looked through the branches, to the twisted trunk. In a flash—and maybe this was the lightning—he understood what Cathal was doing. He saw how the trunk teetered, and how it would fall if knocked off balance.

Brice gripped the rock tight. As the warth climbed, the tree shook, and water from the thinner branches sprayed Brice.

Cathal gave another yell. Brice shut his eyes and grabbed the rock tight, tensing his whole body. The tree groaned. He felt the rock vibrate. The warth let out a desperate roar.

Branches grabbed at Brice, threatening to pull him from the cliff. He forced his head against the rock, his whole body tight, gripping the rock like a limpet. The air was alive with creaks and cracks and sharp, angry splintering, and a strangled roar that faded as the tree fell.

And then there was just the rain washing down over his stinging hands.

He sussed, telling the others he was fine. Then he glanced down to the fallen tree, and to the three warths by the cliff, heads pulled back as they howled in loss. But the sound was too distant to be a threat now.

He turned back to the ledge and climbed.

Ten

Hands grabbed Brice at the ledge, and he let them drag him up. Strange how he felt so tired now.

The ledge stretched about fifteen metres along the cliff. It was wide enough to stand on, then it dipped down into a cave. The roof towered over Brice's head, and water dripped into puddles on the uneven floor, the echoes sharp against the water cascading over the forest.

Brice fought the urge to call out and listen to his voice bounce back. Instead, he followed the others into the cave. It was good to be out of the rain.

"You okay?" Cathal asked, one eyebrow raised. Brice nodded. Cathal looked down to Brice's waist, to his lash.

"The third one was about to attack." What was he supposed to say?

Something slammed into his shoulder, and Brice turned, his fists already clenched. Tris's face was almost in his own, his breath hot and angry.

"What the hell are you trying to do? You could've got us all killed down there!" Tris shook as he pushed hard at Brice's chest. Brice stepped back, just one foot. "You think you could bring a warth down by yourself, you stupid bloody…"

Tris pushed again, but Brice was ready. He blocked with his arm, then brought his own hand up, just like in training. Not the official training, but the sessions at night, when he'd join the few others to learn more useful techniques. His fingers found Tris' throat and squeezed, just enough to let Tris know he could apply more pressure if he wanted to.

"Cut it out!"

A hand came down on Brice's wrist, and Cathal stepped in, between Brice and Tris. He saw Ryann and Keelin behind Tris, pulling him back. Keelin had one of his arms, and Tris struggled against her grip.

"Brice, Tris. No time for this."

Brice released his grip, nodding at Cathal, doing his best to look…not repentant, but accepting. He wasn't the one who had started it, after all.

"Tris, keep yourself in check."

"Hard when you're working with kids!" But Tris only muttered that, turning away when Cathal glared at him.

"And Brice…" Cathal brought his face in close enough for Brice to feel his stale breath. "Brice. You do anything stupid like that again, I'll get you reassigned. We're professionals. We work together. You ignore instructions, you put us all in danger. You understand?"

"But the third warth…"

"I asked a question."

His mouth dry, Brice nodded. "I understand."

"Anything else?"

Brice felt ten years old, and he hated Cathal for that. But he gave the answer his commander expected. "Sorry."

"Learn from this, Brice."

Brice nodded again.

"But he did spot that third warth," Keelin said in a small voice. Brice wanted to smile. But Cathal would think he was being smug, and Tris would get riled again, and…no, best to keep his face straight.

"He did," said Cathal, turning to the rest of the crew. "Doesn't excuse his actions, but he did see it. Ryann?"

"I should've sensed it." Her eyes glazed for a moment. "I can now, but it's weak. Like it's partially protected. Hard to explain."

"It was covered in mud." Brice wondered if any of the others had spotted that. If they'd even bothered to look at the thing.

"Might explain part of it, but not all. No, there's something else. It's…interesting."

Interesting. Not the first word that came to Brice's mind.

"Intentions?" Cathal asked.

"Unclear. There was a nest nearby. But three warths acting together like that is unheard of. And the attack seemed unprovoked. If I had to be pinned down on this, I'd say they were scared. It's worrying."

That was a more appropriate word. But how about freaky, or deadly? How about we need to get the hell out of here?

Cathal must have been thinking something similar. "We need to plan," he said. He turned to look into the cave, then out to the dark clouds rolling over the tree-tops. "So, options. We could take our chances heading for the hold-out, and risk meeting those warths again. We could wait for dawn. Maybe Haven might have thought about sending someone out."

There was a lilt in his voice, and at another time Brice might have laughed. Even if the Proteus had managed to send an automatic update—and with the power playing up, how likely was that?—there was no guarantee Haven would act on it. They trusted crews to fend for themselves.

Keelin closed her eyes, and Brice knew she was trying to reach their Proteus. None of the others said a word, but they all watched the pilot. When she opened her eyes, they were moist. She shook her head.

Ryann placed a hand on Keelin's shoulder, and the look that passed between them could only mean a private suss. Then Ryann turned to Cathal, and Brice knew they, too, were communicating. So much, he thought, for them working together.

"One more option," Cathal said, looking into the cave. "If we're stuck up here, we use our time wisely. We explore. Ryann, brief us."

"We know the cliff's riddled with caves and tunnels, but we have access to no data. That means we have no maps. We go in, we rely on our own intel."

"So, three options," Cathal continued. "Take our chances in the forest, wait for Haven to get round to finding us, or explore the caves. Crew vote. Brice?"

His answer was obvious. They couldn't rely on a rescue, and the forest was damp, depressing and full of warths. And it would be good to see something new for a change. "Caves," he said.

"Tris?"

"I say we wait." He glared at Brice. "Don't want any more accidents."

"Keelin?"

"Best of a bad choice—explore."

"Ryann?"

"Explore. I vote caves."

Cathal nodded. "Vote carried. Tris—how do we go about this?"

Tris scanned the dark depths of the cavern. "We go slow and steady. Just so we don't miss anything. Start here, record everything. Be ready to return," but he stumbled over that word, and it almost came out as 'retreat'. "We don't take any stupid risks."

Brice snorted, but not so loud that any of the others heard him. He knew what Cathal was doing—giving the dissenter a say in what they did—but Tris' response was pretty trite. Go slow, and be ready to run away. About what Brice expected.

But Cathal nodded. "Sound like a plan. Okay, let's do this."

Brice peered into the depths of the cave, searching for the rear wall. Pulling up filters, he saw dark, cold areas that must be passages, and he wondered where they led, and what they held. Not warths, of that he was certain. And it was too dark down here to sustain life—all life needed light, right? He was certain he'd heard that somewhere.

Maybe it was adrenaline from earlier, still running through his body, but for the first time in ages, Brice was excited.

This was adventure. This was exploration. This was what he'd signed up for.

ELEVEN

Ryann kept her frustrations in check. They were entering the unknown, and she needed to remain alert.

But she had made a mistake. She should have sensed that third warth. She should have done more to protect the crew.

And, in truth, she had sensed it, but she'd pushed it to one side. Warths never moved in threes, so she told herself it wasn't a threat. It felt distant, or maybe it was immature. Even if it was close, it wouldn't intrude on the territory of the other two. She'd ignored it, focusing on the immediate danger.

Yet there had been a fourth signal, one that was even less distinct than the third warth. It felt like a sound on the edge of hearing, and nagged at her like an itch that refused to let up. It felt strangely familiar, although it was definitely neither a warth or a person.

It came from the cave. She was certain of that. It felt like the thing was watching, but as they climbed it retreated. And now, as they walked the cave, spaced out in standard formation, all Ryann tasted was a trace that was little more than a hint.

She followed the hint, but the path seemed to double-back, and she caught the flavour from both sides. It hung above her, too, and she imagined a lizard clinging to the rock. But this was no lizard. They were cold-blooded beings, and the flow of the energy in their blood was clear to a tracker. No, this new signal belonged to something that…that possessed a different kind of energy.

Something that was not quite life as she understood it. More of an existence.

Unclear, and troubling. Ryann needed to be careful. She had the crew to keep safe. But she needed more data before she made a firm analysis.

As if on cue, Cathal sussed.

<Thoughts, Ryann, please.>

That was interesting, how he used the word 'please'. She'd noticed how he said it to Keelin earlier, when she'd been trying to raise the Proteus. 'Keep trying, please.' It was something to keep tabs on.

<On the crew?>

<For a start.>

That was ominous. *<They're all coping. Smart move letting Tris lead, by the way.>*

<What about Brice?>

<Over-confident. Should never have slipped on that climb.>

<Agreed. Masked fear or trying to prove himself?>

<Both.>

<Hmm. So what about the third warth?>

Of course, that was what he really wanted to discuss.

<Don't know what I can tell you. The signal was masked, and I was concentrating on the others. I can only apologise.> She didn't feel good lying to him, even if it was only a lie of omission. But Cathal didn't do well with vagueness. She'd tell him when she had something more concrete.

<It was a tense situation. No need to apologise to me, Ryann. Suppose we were fortunate that Brice is so bloody independent.>

<Reminds me of someone else,> she sussed, giving her voice a playful tone.

He paused, as she knew he would. *<I was never that much of a handful.>*

<Of course not.>

He was silent for a moment, then sussed, *<So what do we know of these caves?>*

<Like I said before, not much. The company doesn't see them as a priority.>

<And what about without Kaiahive's crap?>

The use of the name surprised her, especially the way he gave it no inflection. But his use of the word 'crap' gave a better insight into his thoughts. The company was what it was, and he'd deal with that. But he didn't like being kept in the dark.

And his mind was connecting the dots.

<You know as much as me. If you want my thoughts, then yes—there is a chance the cave systems in the cliff reach to the gully. If the missing crew were forced to retreat, we might find them. But it's a long shot.>

<You knew that was on my mind?>

<Thought it was a sensible assumption. Isn't that one of the reasons for this search?>

<Harris, with perception like that, a century ago you'd have been burned as a witch.>

<You've still not quite escaped the backwaters, have you?> Ryann gave her voice a playful lilt, but she knew this was a distraction, and she continued with greater seriousness. *<Anyway, we have no accurate map. We'd be searching blind.>*

<You picking up any life down here?>

It wasn't the question Ryann had expected, and it caught her off-guard. She hated to lie, but … she had to do what was best for the crew. She couldn't encourage unfounded fear or panic.

<Maybe some strains of lichen. But there's no light, so that cuts out most life. If you're looking for monsters in the dark, stick to stories.>

<Suppose that's good to know.> He paused for a moment, and Ryann bit her lip in frustration at the stupidity of her last comment. *<But anything strange, give me a heads-up, right?>*

<Of course.>

Why did she have to mention monsters? It wasn't like she even gave any credence to those rumours.

Of course people muttered about the caves, and what they might contain. It was human nature to populate dark corners with fears. There were those who pushed the company to allow exploratory missions into the caves, if only to reject the fanciful rumours, but Kaiahive refused. Their focus, they said, was on the basin, especially the area closest to Haven.

And, Ryann understood all too clearly, it was in their own interests if the rumours and stories persisted. Stories worked on the mind. They were far more powerful than physical restraints.

Ryann pulled her thoughts back to the cave as they neared the rear wall. She started to analyse, running through some of the data stored in her pack. There was not much that excited her. The rock was a dead thing, dull and uninteresting. The few patches of life clung to the cave entrance, and she ran through the various variants of lichen and moss she'd detected. None of them excited her.

But as they retreated from the entrance, those other traces grew stronger. They had a bitter taste that took her back to her childhood, and her father slaughtering their livestock. Even as a child, she could tell his reasons by the tang in the air. The healthy ones he killed either for sale or for food were lively, their essence struggling to be contained. But the sick ones, and those close to death, had a distinctive flavour that permeated her gut and twisted her stomach. Before she understood her innate abilities, she would blame her father for their suffering, and would refuse to speak to him for days on end.

Now, of course, she understood how he was setting them free from suffering, even though such actions always pained him.

The traces in the cave had a similar flavour. Ryann considered the possibility of a crew carrying a fallen colleague, but she discounted that. She'd have sensed the traces of the healthy ones. She knew no crew apart from her own had set foot in this cave, at least not in the last few days.

"Okay," said Cathal, pulling Ryann from her considerations. "Check your data, then double-log it. Anything worth noting?"

"Just a big empty cave," said Tris, trying to sound confident. His voice was too loud, though, and he flinched at the reverberations.

Data flowed through Ryann. It pushed in from the others, heading straight to the storage in her pack, and at the same time her own data pushed towards Cathal.

"Brice, you ready to send?" Cathal asked. Ryann scanned — Brice's data hadn't transferred automatically.

"Sent it." Brice spoke quietly, and there was confusion in his tone.

Cathal stepped towards Brice. "Hard transfer, just to make sure."

<*Don't single him out,*> Ryann sussed.

"Keelin, Tris, the same. Ryann, we'll triple-log."

He reached out to Brice, placing a hand on the back of his neck, at the lattice's focal node. Then he did the same to Keelin and Tris, before turning to Ryann. His hand was warm and calloused. She felt the data run like liquid.

<*What can you tell me?*> he asked.

<*Brice? Without full diagnosis, I can't say.*> She resisted the urge to run through data.

<*What of the cave? Anything?*>

<*Old trails, but nothing recent.*> He deserved to know that much.

<*Trails of what?*>

<*Too old to tell.*> Then, because he was waiting for more, she added, <*I'm working on it. I'll give you more when I can.*>

He removed his hand, and for a moment her neck was cold. She resisted the impulse to use her own hand to rub some warmth back into it. Instead she shrugged her pack higher.

"Okay," Cathal said, sweeping a hand round at the rock. "Three tunnels. Any thoughts?"

"This one," Tris said, pointing to the left. "It's the biggest. Don't want to be all crouched over."

The tunnel was biggest, but the floor was uneven and stony, in contrast to the smooth undulations of the cave itself. To Ryann that indicated a tunnel underused.

"Smaller one might be more interesting, though." Brice pointed to the middle route, and from the lift at the corners of his mouth, Ryann knew he was making this suggestion only to push Tris. The tunnel was more of a hole, no higher than her thigh. It looked like the hole rose sharply, so they'd be climbing as well as crawling.

"Keelin?" Cathal asked, and Ryann realised how little she had heard from the pilot.

"I'm not good at this." She shrugged, and looked away. The loss of the Proteus was hitting Keelin hard.

<*You still in contact with the craft, Kee?*> Ryann sussed. The use of 'Kee' was important here, she felt.

<*Too faint. And it will only get worse the deeper we go.*>

And yet Keelin had chosen to explore the caves.

<*We'll be fine,*> Ryann told her. <*The Proteus isn't going anywhere.*>

"Ryann?" Cathal asked.

She focused on the trails, and followed them. Some climbed into the hole, and more used the larger path. But the majority filled the path to the right. The rock on the ground was smooth, although this spread to the walls, and so Ryann doubted it was from the tread of many feet. It was more likely that this tunnel had been carved by water.

One of the other foundations of life, she thought. The moss and lichen clung to the edges of the cave, where they could pull moisture from the air, and drink heavily from the rain that streaked the rock. If whatever left these traces could survive with reduced light, it would still need water. So this tunnel made sense.

"This one," she said, and might have justified her decision, but Cathal nodded instantly.

"Okay," he said. "Everyone, keep recording. We travel slow. Capture anything of interest and broadcast. Ryann, you're on point."

She nodded, and stepped into the tunnel.

In the confined space, the trace was stronger, and the death stench a constant background note. She ran a hand over the rock, imagining how water once flowed over it.

Follow the water, she told herself. It must have come from above. And whatever left that trace would need to drink. Follow the water to find life.

But a small voice at the back of her mind told her that life needed more than water.

It also needed to feed.

Twelve

Cathal felt better when he was moving. Always had done. Sitting down made him think of paperwork, and that pushed him into apathy. But when he walked, blood flowed better, and his thoughts moved faster.

Ryann was holding out on him. Not lying exactly, but covering up her thoughts. Cathal could go through her data, but she was smart. He knew how she could hide the important stuff in plain view. He'd look too deep, and he'd miss what she really thought.

He checked his emotions. His annoyance wasn't with Ryann, or with any of the others. True, Tris was wimping out, Keelin was retreating, and Brice was a whole swarm of concerns. But Cathal could deal with that. Easier than playing politics back at Haven.

No, he was annoyed at the situation. And, yes, the lies—no, misinformation—Kaia-bloody-hive had fed him.

There was the missing crew, for starters. The mission briefing said they were to check out irregular signals picked up by a long-range drone. That was it. No details on these signals, and no indication of how the crew should respond. Usually, something that far from Haven, there were strict protocols—search in half-hour bursts, feed back reports regularly, only split up in certain, pre-defined situations, yadda yadda yadda. The mission briefings were usually full of bullet-points some desk-jockey on Metis had vomited up.

But the briefing for this mission had none of that.

When Cathal dug deeper—and he hated having to call in a favour from Piran, that slimy bottom-feeder—he was surprised at how quickly the crew were dispatched. And how little additional information they were given. Nothing about the spread or nature of these signals. Or about the dead warth, further along the gully. According to the drone's data, there was no sign of broken bones, so a fall seemed unlikely. There was a deep wound in its neck, but little blood.

The crew's commander was Nels Kollias, and although Cathal didn't know him well, he knew of the man's reputation. Solid, but he wasn't one to work hard. He wouldn't have dug any deeper. He wouldn't have a clue about the warth.

He'd led his crew blindly into the gully, searching for something capable of killing a warth.

Cathal had no doubts that Nels had led his crew to their deaths. His own mission wasn't search-and-rescue, but recovery of assets.

If Kaiahive expected him to lead his crew as blindly as Nels did, they had another thing coming. Screw the mission—crew always came first.

But he wasn't sure this lot were up to it. Oh, they weren't a bad bunch, but they were too young. Kids. Keelin was a great pilot, maybe one of the best he'd seen, but she was still wet behind the ears. Separated from the Proteus, she was dead weight. And Tris—the lad was a genius with tech. Cathal got that. But he'd be better off in Haven, or even back on Metis. He wasn't cut out for action.

Then there was Brice. The most troublesome of the three, undoubtedly, but also the one with the greatest potential. Ryann might have been ribbing him earlier, but Cathal did see some of himself in the greenest of the crew. The defiance of authority, the disdain for others—dangerous attitudes, but in small doses Cathal knew they gave an edge where it mattered. Like earlier, when Brice had fired his lash. Yes, it was a bloody stupid thing to do, and Cathal had to hold himself back from ripping the kid to shreds over it. But he'd seen a threat, and he'd responded. He'd taken the initiative.

But if his lattice was playing up, he'd lose that edge. Cathal didn't want to be carrying more dead weight. This wasn't going to be a stroll in the park.

Ryann led them along tunnels that, to Cathal, seemed too smooth. And the roof was too low. He would have preferred the larger passage, but even then he knew he wouldn't feel settled. He didn't like the thought of having so much rock over his head, just waiting to come down.

If it happened, he hoped it would be quick. Better a sudden, final blow to the head than a drawn-out death in a sealed tomb.

<I'm getting something,> Ryann sussed. Meaning she was willing to talk about what she already had.

<Go on.>

<Not sure what it is, but definitely animal. It's come this way.>

<We following it?>

<We're following one of its routes. I can't say when it passed, though.>

Cathal almost asked if she meant 'won't' instead of 'can't'. Instead, he sussed, *<Suggestions?>*

<You wanted data. It's something new. Maybe we track it.>

That was too vague, even for Ryann. And she was choosing her words with too much care.

<Sounds good. Follow the trail, Ryann.>

The newbies were oblivious to this, and Cathal watched them trudge along, scanning to the left and right. Only Brice looked up, he noticed. Seemed to be a little unsteady when he did so, but at least the lad was keeping his wits about him.

Not that there was much to see, even with night-vision filters. Ryann pushed through the black, and it was like the darkness opened for them, only to close up behind Cathal. He saw it enveloping them, like some malignancy. They were a bubble in the depths, only surviving because nature let them. And nature was ever-fickle.

Oh, hell—he was getting all fancy. He shook his head to clear his thoughts. He'd put all that garbage behind him. Facts—that was what mattered. Leave the poetry to the old and the weak.

The rock was further from his head now. And the tunnel became a long, narrow chamber. There was a narrow ledge some five metres up, and Cathal saw dark patches that he was certain were holes. How far back they went, he couldn't say.

<*This place look strange to anyone?*> he sussed, wide. The familiar dryness in his mouth told him something wasn't right.

Ryann slowed her pace, following his implied instruction.

<*Interesting,*> she sussed, in the tone of someone who had far more to add. But she said no more.

<*That ledge looks too even,*> Keelin sussed, and Cathal saw Tris nod in agreement.

<*Those more tunnels up there?*> Tris asked.

<*Let's check this out.*>

The tunnel was about five metres across now, and the crew spread out, then formed a circle. At least they'd all paid attention to his training.

<*Okay. We take a couple of minutes. Investigate, analyse, then report. No need to move.*>

They started to scan. He'd trained them well, even though they were rough round the edges. But what could you expect after a few months? The last crew, he'd held together for over a year.

But now wasn't the time to think of that.

He ran his own hand over the rock—undulating and grainy, like it had been filed down, and not simply water-eroded. Yet above the ledge Cathal saw cracks and bulges, the kind of thing he'd expect from rock. And the roof, way over their heads, was far from smooth.

Cathal didn't know the exact make-up of this rock, but if there were stalactites, shouldn't there be corresponding stalagmites? As water dripped from above, it must land. Yet the ground was as smooth as the lower part of the wall.

It wasn't natural. It couldn't be.

He focused on the ledge, then glanced across to the opposite wall. There was a matching ledge, with more holes. And higher up, a second ledge, only that one was more ragged, or maybe it was less manufactured.

<Think we might have company.>

Ryann's voice was a sharp whisper, and Cathal instantly dropped his stance, knees bent and legs ready. One hand rested near his lash, although he knew he wouldn't draw it. Not yet.

<Where?>

The others copied his stance, although only Brice fell into it naturally. The lad's head moved slowly, whereas the others jerked one way then another, and their eyes were too wide.

<Up on the ledge, some twenty metres back. I think...I think it's been following us.>

No, Cathal thought. You don't think, you know. You've been tracking it.

She should have mentioned it earlier.

He looked behind, pulling up filters. But he caught nothing.

<Which side?>

<Our left as we walked in.>

He still couldn't see anything. Whatever Ryann had sensed must be hiding. Unless she was mistaken. But Cathal didn't believe that.

<A warth?>

<Tris, when we return to Haven, remind me to put you back in the remedial program. You see any trees down here?>

It was wrong to snap, but goddamn that kid could be dense at times, especially for someone so bright.

But if it wasn't a warth—which it wasn't—what was it?

<What do we do?> sussed Ryann, privately.

<You say it's been around for a while?>

<It's hard to say. Maybe.>

That was too vague for comfort. *<So it's wary. That could be good.>* Then he opened communication up wide. *<We treat this like we treat the warths. No sudden movement, no threats. And let's see if it is following us. Ryann, lead on.>*

There was a slight hesitation before she nodded, turned, and walked slowly away. The others fell into line behind her, keeping to the dead centre of the path.

<Tell me everything,> he sussed to Ryann.

<*Still there. Hasn't moved. Oh, now it has. But not along the ledge.*>

<*Explain.*>

<*Sensed it at one of the holes, but now it's at the next hole along.*>

<*Any sense of structure beyond the holes?*>

<*Can't do rock. You know that.*>

So it was up to inference and logic. The thing moved from hole to hole without using the ledge, which meant the holes were connected. Most feasible explanation—a second tunnel, running behind the ledge.

And, again, that couldn't be natural. Especially not when the holes seemed too evenly spaced. Like observation posts, or some strange theatre.

<*It's jumped.*>

What did she mean by that? <*Explain.*>

<*It's on our right now.*>

<*Not a different one?*> If the ledge to the right also gave access to a tunnel, how many of these…these whatevers were hiding up there?

<*Pretty sure it's the same one.*>

The distance between the ledges was pushing ten metres now. Was it possible for something to jump that gap without making a sound?

<*What the hell is it?*>

<*No idea.*> Her response was too fast, like she was covering up her true thoughts.

<*Keep moving,*> he sussed, his own pace bringing him closer to Brice. The lad was scanning, but he was keeping his nerves in check. More so than either Keelin or Tris. Neither of them moved smoothly. Worryingly, Tris had his lash drawn.

<*Tris, holster that thing.*>

The lad looked down, almost surprised, then holstered the weapon. His hand shook without something to occupy it.

<*It's back on the left,*> Ryann sussed.

<*Jumped again? You sure?*>

She paused. <*Positive.*>

<*Any more of them?*> The words sounded weak. Any more of what?

<*Can't feel any. But that doesn't mean it's alone.*>

That was no comfort at all.

So, analyse. The ledges were ten metres up, with smooth rock that offered no clear climb. But—if he trusted Ryann on this—their watcher could leap a distance like that. And there was no certainty it was on its own. They didn't know what lay beyond the holes.

Cathal had insufficient data to form a clear assessment. He wasn't going to make the same mistake as Nels.

<*Okay,*> he sussed wide. <*We've gone as far as we need to. We head back to the cave and reassess.*>

He could feel the relief flowing from the crew.

<*You want me on point again?*> Already Ryann was moving round the others.

<*I've got the route mapped. I'll lead. You keep a trace on our friend.*>

That didn't come across as light as he intended, and he doubted the smile helped. But she nodded and took a step back, behind Keelin.

<*Okay, let's go. Keep watch, keep recording.*>

He turned, pushing his fears deep down. If the thing had been following them, they were now approaching it. But there was no avoiding this. Without a map, they had to retrace their steps.

Fifteen minutes, and he'd see the open air again.

Even the bloody rain would be pleasant after this.

He looked up to the roof. For a moment nausea rose, and his vision swam. He shut his eyes and brought his head back down. This place was getting to him. At least on the Proteus he could call up external sensors and pretend he was outside. But down here, not even the air moved. It was like a tomb; stuffy and dead.

But it was logical to explore. They had part of the tunnels mapped now, even if it was only a small part. And they knew of another creature. That would surely be of interest to the company. That might make up for failing to find the missing crew.

The tunnel narrowed, the walls closing in, green-tinged in his filters. The roof would be lower, too. He could sense the weight of the rock above him.

Cathal glanced up, one arm out to balance. He saw the ledge, and the shadows.

His vision swirled as the shadows moved, and darkness crashed down on him.

Thirteen

Brice heard a yell as the black shape fell on Cathal. The man disappeared, pinned down by shadowy limbs. A howl cut through the air, and Brice saw a mouth, wide and black, lined with fangs. The mouth jerked sharply, and the fangs vanished into the shadows as Cathal screamed in agony.

Brice dropped to a crouch and raised his lash, crosshairs ready. He heard voices; curses and yells, maybe instructions. He pulled up more filters, desperate to see into the shadows. To see what he was aiming at.

There was a crack, and the air by Brice's head surged forwards with an ozone blast. For a moment his vision burst with light, and a deep rolling roar filled his ears. There was more shouting. Brice shouted too, waving his lash in the air, and only now realising he could no longer see the sights. Or anything else.

<*What's happening?*> he cried out. Maybe one of the shouts was an answer. He couldn't tell.

Something barrelled into him, forcing him back. Brice threw his free hand forward, and it struck something leathery and cold.

There was a dry, rasping hiss in his ears, and a coppery, rancid stench smothered his face. He felt warm splashes on his skin, and he didn't want to know what they were.

Brice brought his lash up and forward, and when it met resistance he pushed harder. Whatever was there pushed back, and

Brice squeezed the trigger. For a moment he felt a call to his lattice, requesting targeting, but the call was too far away, and he repeated the squeeze, going into automatic manual override. He felt the surge of energy, and then his arm flew backwards, twisting his body.

When his head struck the rock, nausea raced through him as a brilliantly dark light flared and died.

Then he was on the floor and he could hear heavy, trembling breathing.

"What the hell was that thing?" Tris screamed.

The roar in his ears became the background drone of pumping blood, and other sounds reached him. He heard steps, and a gasp. There was the soft rustling of fabric, then something tearing. He could smell sweat, and blood, and something sharp and acrid that left a sour taste in his mouth. He wanted to vomit.

And he still could not see.

Brice called up his lattice, scanning for filters. But he couldn't find them. He saw the usual options, but they faded and slipped away when he reached out. He blinked hard, holding his eyes shut tight and then releasing, but still nothing. His eyes itched, like they used to when he first had the lenses implanted.

His shoulder throbbed. The lash had been on full power —without looking, and without confirmation from his lattice, he knew he'd thumbed the intensity as far as it would go. He knew there would be kick-back from such a blast, especially at point blank range, but it shouldn't have been so harsh and uncontrolled. His lattice should have compensated.

Brice reached a hand round to his neck, searching for some kind of sign, like the usual flare of heat beneath his skin's surface. But he found nothing.

There were more sounds now, maybe a few metres from his feet. Someone was tapping, or maybe it was tools or some other kind of equipment. But he couldn't hear voices. Hadn't done since Tris cried out in fright.

<Anyone?> he called out. *<Cathal? You okay? Keelin? Ryann? Hey, Tris, you need a change of underwear yet?>*

Nothing.

Pain jolted through his thigh, like someone had kicked him. It wasn't hard, but Brice winced anyway.

"You staying there or what?"

That was Tris, and he was standing over Brice. He sounded out of breath.

"You need to kick me?"

There was no response, but Brice heard more steps. He felt pressure on his arm, and was about to pull away when fingers squeezed.

"You okay, Brice?" said Keelin, and she sounded close, like she was right by his side.

"Don't know. It just me, or is it dark down here?"

Again, there was no response. Then Keelin spoke again.

"Did you hear that?"

"What?"

"Any of it." She paused. "Did you hear what Tris called you?"

Brice took a breath. He suddenly realised how cold it was.

"I haven't heard anything since…since whatever the hell happened."

"Did you see it come for you?"

"See what come for me?" Something leathery, with foul breath and a stomach that could withstand a blast from a lash.

"It ran right into you. I thought…we thought you were going to be next."

"Next?"

There was another pause. Another part of a conversation that did not include Brice.

"Can you walk?"

Brice nodded, assuming Keelin could see him, and rose to his feet. His legs were fine, if a little shaky, but he swayed, and might have fallen if not for Keelin's grip. He brought a hand up to his head, feeling the tenderness to one side, where it had struck the rock. His fingers came away damp.

"Can't see where I'm going, though."

"I'll guide you." Her hand moved to his elbow, and another reached across onto his forearm.

"Brice, you ready?" This was Ryann's voice, and she sounded more distant than usual. If that was possible.

"Sure. What for?"

"We're leaving. Tris, you want to get Cathal with me?"

What was up with Cathal? That was the only voice he hadn't heard.

"Let's go."

The tone was wrong. Cathal's voice was gruff and sounded disinterested. But Ryann's voice was light and uncertain. It didn't sound right, Ryann giving the order.

In the darkness, Brice shuffled, trusting Keelin to guide him. He had no other choice.

"So what happened?" he asked.

Maybe her fingers twitched on his forearm. "Not yet. Let's get out first."

She squeezed his arm. Brice felt that, but only through his jacket. He received no message from his lattice, and couldn't isolate the synapses that had been triggered. It was like his lattice was no longer keeping him informed.

And the noises around him were off, too. He heard boots striking rock, but the sound was smothered, like his ears were stuffed with cotton wool. He couldn't even distinguish individual treads, not even Tris' normal clomping. When Brice counted the sounds, he thought he heard five sets, but the muffled echoes confused him.

Keelin pulled Brice's arm back, and they stopped. "Tunnel's narrower here," she said. "Put your hands on my shoulders. And try not to step on my ankles."

She took one of his hands and placed it on her shoulder. Water oozed out as he pressed down. He hoped she wasn't this wet inside, and then realised that was a stupid thing to think. They'd been in the water—of course she was soaked. But her jacket would be helping, along with her lattice. It would be keeping her warm.

He shivered again, cold seeping into his whole body. His jaw shook, and he knew that if he relaxed it his teeth would start chattering. He didn't want Keelin to hear that.

"Keep your other hand out," she said, "and your head low. We'll take it slow."

"Okay." Then thinking he should say something else, he added, "Thanks." It didn't seem enough, but he could imagine her smile.

"Let's go."

He shuffled on, one hand running over rock. He hunched over, his head forward. He could smell something…not exactly fresh, but comforting, and he realised this must be Keelin. He tried to picture her. Hair fell over her collar, but he couldn't remember if it was dark or light, and he felt bad about that. He tried to remember the colour of her eyes. But they were usually half-hidden by her hair, so how was he supposed to notice details like that?

He should have been able to call up an image from his data store.

Brice's neck felt sore. He assumed that was down to the angle at which he held his head, but he wasn't sure if his neck muscles were cold or warm. He took his hand from the chilled rock and placed it on his skin, just beneath his hairline, and he rubbed.

He needed to attempt a reboot.

Brice took a breath and delved inside, thinking of a pattern he'd been shown and told to remember. The sequence wasn't numbers or letters. That might appeal to someone data-driven like Tris, or even Keelin, but Brice needed something more physical. His sequence involved…levers, that was it.

He saw them now, in a dingy, dust-thick hut with no windows. The levers themselves reached up to his chest, and sat in a frame that was not as rusty as it should have been, although the paint was peeling in long, sharp flakes.

He grabbed the first lever in the sequence, the furthest to his left, and pulled. He tightened his arm and leaned out, using his body weight, and the lever moved with a grinding creak. Then it clicked into place, just before it hit the frame.

Brice moved on to the next in the sequence, then the third, running through the pattern without thinking now. Seven levers, because seven was a good number for memory. Or so he'd been told.

The final lever was the central one. The rubber on the handle was starting to perish from years of sweat and neglect. He grasped it, feeling rough edges around the smoothness, and he pulled. The lever moved with a metal-on-metal grinding that set Brice's teeth on edge, and when it slammed into place the pressure yanked at his shoulders.

For a moment, nothing happened. A few dust motes flickered as they fell to the ground.

And then his skin ignited as a million flames danced beneath the surface. The fire tore along neurons and blood vessels, a surge of intense power flooding through him. Every synapse fired, his limbs jerking rigid, and for a fraction of a second Brice could feel every single cell in his body, a torrent of data that flared and burnt out with a magnesium after-burn that made his eyeballs itch.

He must have clenched the hand on Keelin's shoulder, because she gasped, and he saw her head twitch.

He saw her.

Her hair hung in night-vision green tendrils, and her jacket was a deeper shade, stark against the surrounding rock. Brice looked down, and he saw her boots, with one lace starting to slip free. Then he saw—and felt—her turn. Her eyes might have only been green because of his filters, but they looked at him.

He smiled. "Back on-line," he said. The words felt anti-climactic, but they'd do.

She nodded, like it was the most common thing in the world. "So we can go a bit faster now?" She turned her head, and he caught her message to the others. *<Brice can see again.>*

<Good. Maybe we can get out before that thing comes back.>

Brice had never been so pleased to hear voices in his head. Even Tris' angry tone couldn't drag him down.

The tunnel roof wasn't as low as Brice had imagined, and he straightened up. He could see over Keelin's shoulder now, but what he saw didn't make sense.

He reached for more filters. Many were unresponsive, and he couldn't zoom in, so he had to focus manually.

Tris and Ryann walked at an angle, not quite sideways but twisted. At first Brice couldn't make out why, but then he saw Cathal between them, his arms round their shoulders. They each had hold of a hand, and Cathal's head hung down, lolling between them. His eyes were closed. His boots dragged along the ground.

And the side of his jacket was covered in a dark stain. There was a discoloured bandage on his shoulder and neck. Part of the tape was already coming loose, and Brice saw liquid oozing round it.

<Cathal?> Brice sussed, reaching out. He wasn't surprised when there was no response.

Maybe if he had tracker training, like Ryann, he could reach out and feel Cathal's lattice.

But he didn't need to do that to know his commander's condition was serious. His skin was pale. He was unconscious, and bleeding.

Brice shivered, and this time it wasn't because of the cold.

FOURTEEN

They walked in silence. Brice kept his eyes on Keelin, directly in front of him. He didn't want to look any further.

And then the air moved across his face. It carried a fragrance that brushed away the staleness of the tunnels, a staleness he hadn't been aware of, but now realised had been all-encompassing, like the rock pressing in. He drew the aroma in—damp leaves, and something vaguely compost-like.

The others must have felt this too, because they increased their pace. And when they rounded the next corner, and the cavern opened up, cool refreshing air rushed over them, and to Brice it felt like life itself. He took a long, deep pull, and then ran towards the lip, jumping up the rock, barely brushing it with his hands. He lifted his head and looked to the sky, water spraying his face and trickling into his mouth. He'd never tasted anything so good.

<*Thanks for the help, Brice!*>

Tris' suss dripped with angry sarcasm, and Brice turned to see him and Ryann dragging Cathal across the cave, boots scuffing on the ground. They reached the base of the lip and set him down, easing him into a sitting position.

Brice climbed down to join them, avoiding Tris' eyes. Data-boy was just being pathetic. Brice would only have got in the way.

Besides, Tris wasn't the one whose lattice had shut down, or who had that thing push into him. He needed to man up.

Ryann was by Cathal, crouched down, reaching for his neck. Brice watched, a step back. Cathal's eyes, still closed, flickered.

<*Keelin, the kit and another bandage from my pack? Thanks.*>

Ryann's fingers found the edge of the bandage, and she pulled it free. The sodden material came away with a sucking sound. The wound was deep. Through the crimson, Brice saw what he imagined must be tendons and, far down, something solid that might have been white.

The wound reached down to his bone.

Ryann took the medikit from Keelin, opened it and removed a vial that she attached to a needle-less syringe. She held the syringe over Cathal's wound.

<*Hold him. All of you.*>

They did as Ryann asked, Tris on one side, Keelin on the other. Brice dropped to the man's legs, placing a hand on each ankle.

As Ryann pressed the plunger and the liquid splashed into the wound, Brice struggled to keep his grip. Cathal's whole body buckled violently. Tris cursed under his breath. The shaking intensified. Brice twisted his body to lay across Cathal's spasming legs.

Ryann placed a clean bandage over the wound. She ripped off the side tabs and stuck it into place. Cathal shuddered, spittle flying as his head rocked violently.

<*Few more seconds.*>

The shaking subsided, and Briced eased off Cathal's legs. He didn't know if the warmth was from him or Cathal. But the man was still now, and he looked strangely at peace. Ryann had one hand on his forehead. Brice assumed this was some medical thing.

"What now?" he asked.

<*So much for silence.*>

Brice shot Tris a look. Tris sneered in return.

<*You hearing us?*>

Brice turned to Ryann and nodded. <*At the moment. This getting through?*>

"But you'd prefer to talk?" she said. He wasn't sure if she'd heard his suss or not.

"I'd prefer to be back in Haven."

"Think we all would." Ryann looked down to Cathal. She opened her mouth, like she was about to say something, then shook her head.

Rain fell on trees outside, and water dripped from the roof of the cave. The storm rumbled on. For a while, those were the only sounds. When Ryann spoke again, her voice was stronger.

"Keelin, anything from the Proteus?"

Keelin's eyes glazed for a moment. She swallowed, her throat bobbing, and shook her head. Ryann's face softened. Then she climbed up to the cave entrance, scanning the forest below. Her hands wavered by her side, before she placed them on her hips.

"Let's talk this through." Ryann turned, and her eyes dipped towards Cathal. "Options."

"How serious…I mean, what's wrong with him?" Tris said.

"Unsure. Wound's deep, and the healing's not taking like it should. Probably a toxin. Nothing I've come across before." Her chest rose and fell between each sentence, like she was squeezing the words out.

"Call for help?" Brice suggested, but he knew it was the wrong thing to say when Tris snorted.

Ryann held up a hand. "Tris, try."

"Won't work," he said, shrugging the pack from his back and unzipping a pocket. Brice recognised the box he produced as a relay, something that would boost a signal. Tris played with it, his head shaking the whole time. "Nowhere near a strong enough signal. I can read the Proteus, but power's too weak to ride. And the storm's not helping."

"Nyle and Osker?" Tris looked confused for a moment, so she refreshed his memory. "You said they were at a hold-out nearby."

Tris was still for a moment, then shook his head again. "Nothing."

Ryann's lips smacked in annoyance. "We can't stay here. Nearest hold-out's ninety minutes." She glanced at Cathal again. "Probably take longer."

"Warths?" Brice recalled how Cathal hadn't been keen to head back into the forest.

Tris put the relay back in his pack and hoisted it onto his shoulders. "Oh, yeah. The ones Brice got all riled for us. How about we send him out as an offering? About all he's good for."

"How about you go down first, you're so tough."

"At least I haven't screwed things up for us."

"Haven't done anything useful either."

"Stop!"

Ryann rarely raised her voice, and it was like a slap to Brice's face. She continued, in her usual tone. "Focus on the problem."

"Can you sense the warths, Ryann?" Keelin asked. "They still upset?"

Ryann closed her eyes. "They've moved off, but not far. One of them is in pain. Hard to tell how they'll react."

That would be the one climbing the tree, or maybe the one Brice had caught with his lash. He waited for some comeback from Tris, but there was none. And he wasn't going to say anything. If Tris wanted to be childish about this, that was his outlook. Brice was better than that.

"So we head for the hold-out?" He desperately wanted Ryann to give a positive reply. But Tris spoke first.

"You really want to face those things again, Brice?"

"You want to hang around for whatever comes out of those tunnels?" Brice raised a hand as emphasis. Data-boy glanced towards the back of the cave and swallowed.

"So how do we get Cathal down?" Keelin asked. Brice hadn't noticed her move, but now she stood on the lip, dark clouds behind her, a boot nudging a protruding boulder.

And that gave Brice an idea. The rock was uneven, and his eyes followed a number of cracks. He thought of the kit in his pack.

He walked forward, inspecting the rock, and climbed up next to Keelin. Just behind her, where the cliff fell away, the edge was smooth. Brice leaned forward and looked down to the soil below. He calculated the distance.

“You got something, Brice?” Ryann asked.

“We climb.” The solution was obvious.

“You going to carry Cathal, then?” Tris snorted, and muttered something under his breath.

Brice shrugged off his pack, and pulled out the micro-rope. It was barely the width of his little finger, but he’d used it before. He knew how strong it was.

“We lower him.” He smiled, and noticed how Tris avoided his eyes. “I can set up a system, no problem. If we…I don’t know, strap his arms and legs up, maybe wrap his head. I’ve done it in training. I can lower him.”

“So we feed him to the warths? You’re an animal, Brice.”

“They’re further off,” Ryann said.

“But still around, right?” Tris turned to Ryann, taking a step forward. “We only just made it away from them last time. We go down there, and who knows what’s going to happen?”

Tris’ face was inches from hers, and Brice realised he’d never seen Tris squaring up like this, not to Ryann. But she remained impassive. She met his gaze and held it.

“We don’t know what will happen if we stay, either,” she said. “And he needs help.” She pointed towards Cathal, but continued to stare at Tris.

He stepped back, then looked down. “But the warths are still down there somewhere,” he said quietly.

“So we need to be vigilant,” Brice said, the plan forming as he spoke. “We need someone on the ground first. We lower Cathal, and the rest of us follow.”

“And what if the warths return?” There wasn’t the same anger in Tris’ voice now. It had been replaced by a pleading tone.

“We pull him back up, and whoever’s already down there climbs.”

“What if we’re all down there?”

In the stillness that followed Tris’ question, Brice turned away and listened. He could still make out the background of the rain in the trees, and the constant rumble from the storm. In the back of the cavern dripping water echoed.

"What if that thing comes back while we wait, Tris?" Keelin asked. "At least we know about warths. At least…" She glanced at Cathal and seemed unable to finish.

"We go," Ryann said, looking at each of them in turn. When she caught Brice's eyes, he thought that maybe she smiled. "Lesser of two evils. But we need someone good on the ground. Tris?"

His head shook once, then nodded. "I can do that," he said, trying to convince himself.

"And Keelin, you climb down with Cathal. That gives us extra hands on the ground should anything happen. I'll call if I sense anything." Brice wasn't sure if she was talking about the warths or the thing in the cave. "Brice, how long to set up?"

"Five minutes. Loads of good placements."

"Get on it. Keelin, set up a sling for Cathal. Lots of padding. Tris, get ready to climb."

Brice saw both Keelin and Tris nod. Ryann glanced at Cathal, then stood straight, hands on her hips. Her voice was sharp and loud.

"Okay. Let's do this."

FIFTEEN

Ryann fractured her mind, segmenting everything that was happening. She saw Brice set up the belay system, and noted his efficiency. She saw how Tris took deep breaths up on the lip, and knew he was struggling to keep his fear in check. She saw Keelin use webbing to build a body-harness for Cathal, and noticed with interest the tenderness with which she moved his body.

And she allowed her lattice to reach out to Cathal. She pushed into his own lattice, forcing herself on when it kicked back, even though she knew the dangers of this. But she needed to know what was happening. She needed to understand.

Blood still leaked from his wound. He had lost about a half-litre, maybe a little more. Not a great amount for such a wound, and Ryann had to assume that was down to his lattice. It would be doing everything it could to keep Cathal alive.

But it was working too hard. Energy raged through his body. Neurons fired too fast, and his muscles twitched on a cellular level almost constantly. Ryann knew Cathal's body could not sustain that kind of intensity. Sooner or later, his muscles would start to atrophy, and neurons would start misfiring more often. If nothing changed, his own body would work against him.

She needed to get him back to Haven, but even then, she could think of little the medical team could do. They could artificially pump more plasma around his body, and they could control the temperature of his environment. They could keep him alive. But she couldn't see how they could reverse the damage.

She couldn't see any future for Cathal.

But they had to try. And they had to get away from this cave.

She watched Brice and Keelin lift Cathal into position, and she gave Tris a nod. He returned it, pushing his fear down, and started to climb.

And Ryann turned her attention to the rear of the cave, where the creature hid in the shadows and watched them.

Its signal was elusive, and her lattice seemed to slip around it. But she'd felt it, even as they brought Cathal back to this cave. She didn't know when it returned, just that it was there, keeping back. It followed them.

But it didn't attack. Ryann didn't know what that meant.

She pushed towards it. She couldn't detect movement now, and it almost merged with the lifeless rock. She might have described this as stillness, or calm, but it felt more like a void.

Ryann heard Tris saying he was down, and she pushed into the forest.

<Warths are a long way off, Tris. Should have no problems.>

<Good to know. Thanks.>

She looked over to Brice and Keelin, and gave them the nod. As they shuffled Cathal to the edge—something she didn't want to watch, even though she trusted Brice's rope-work—she returned her attention to the creature in the shadows.

It was unlike anything she'd come across before, even in the virtual scenarios in training. Yet there was a familiarity about it, something she felt she should be able to grasp. But it evaded her every time she pushed—not like it was actively rejecting her, but more like…she didn't know what it was like.

She didn't know anything about it. And that scared the hell out of Ryann.

<We're down,> Keelin sussed. Brice dismantled his rope system. Ryann wanted to tell him to leave it, that they needed to get down as quickly as possible. But the creature was not making a move.

Yet it stirred. There was a shift in its position, almost like it knew they would soon be gone.

Was that what it wanted? Had they crossed into its territory, and it only attacked to repel them? That would make sense, but only if she ignored how it had bitten down on Cathal and...yes, she had to accept this...sucked at the wound.

Like it was feeding.

"Ready," Brice said, shouldering his pack. "You want to climb first?"

Ryann shook her head. She should be at the rear. But she didn't want to be alone with that thing up here.

"There's enough space to climb together," she said, trying to make that sound like a logical solution rather than the act of a coward.

They climbed. Ryann didn't enjoy this, but she could climb without struggling, and that meant she could keep focused on the creature.

As they dropped over the edge, it emerged from the tunnel entrance. She couldn't feel its motion, but she could sense its void shift, and something sparked. Interest, or intelligence. Something vital, at odds with the dark cloud that surrounded the creature.

It reached the lip as her feet found soil—wonderful, moist soil, with all its sensations of life—but it came no further. It didn't reach the cliff itself. Almost as if it didn't want to get too close to the open air.

<*What now?*> Keelin asked. The pilot had propped Cathal against the cliff, and was holding him steady, one hand on his shoulder. Tris was on the man's other side, but he kept his eyes on the trees—either watching for warths or avoiding looking at Cathal. Brice was a few paces away, and he alternated between looking into the trees and glancing up at the cliff.

What now? What would Cathal do?

He'd make sure the crew was safe. He'd formulate a plan, and they'd follow it. And, Ryann realised, they had a plan—get to the closest hold-out. It wasn't much of a plan, but it was better than nothing.

She took a breath, looked into the trees—no warths nearby, which was a comfort—then back to Keelin.

"We walk." But she needed to say more, and she thought how Cathal would organise things. "I'm on point. Keelin next. Tris, you've got the rear." That was an important position, and the extra responsibility might keep him focused. "Brice?"

He turned, and she saw him glance at Cathal. "You want me to carry him?" There was a hint of resentment in his voice.

"Can you manage that?"

"Sure." He shrugged his pack off. "Might work if he's strapped to my back, though. He already has a harness on. Keelin, give me a hand?"

Ryann wanted to smile at that, at the way he was stepping up. But another part of her knew she should have been the one to give the instructions. Cathal would have done that. Even if the idea had come from Brice, Cathal would have been in control.

"Get on it. We move off as soon as we can." And, again, that sounded weak.

<*Tris,*> she sussed privately, <*When we move, I want you to watch our backs. You detect anything, tell me. Keep communications tight.*>

He stood straighter now. <*I can do that. Sure you don't want me to keep the others informed?*>

<*No. You tell me everything, I'll decide if it's a risk.*> She chose her words with care, knowing Tris needed every boost to his confidence she could give him. She needed to appeal to his ego. <*I don't want to make them nervous. We need to keep things calm.*>

He nodded, a hint of a smile on his lips.

Yes, that was how Cathal did it. He pulled at strengths to cover weaknesses. He used whatever he could, and he got the crew working together.

She turned to look at Brice. He wore Cathal like a back-pack, tight against his body. Keelin had used webbing to strap the man in place, and even his head was bound to Brice's shoulder.

"You okay with my pack?" he asked Keelin. Ryann noticed how she wore it across her chest, her own pack on her back.

"It's fine. Not as much weight as you're carrying."

Brice flexed his shoulders. "Feels good. No slippage." He smiled.

"Okay," Ryann said, suppressing her own smile. "Let's do this."

She led the crew into the trees, and she almost felt confident.

SIXTEEN

Movement felt good to Brice, even with the extra weight he carried. Maybe because of it. He felt his legs pushing harder, and the warmth was a comfort. Even his breathing, deeper with each step, felt good.

Almost good enough to ignore the fact that, once again, he was doing the donkey work.

But he could understand why things needed to be this way. Keelin could never have managed to carry Cathal like this, and Ryann needed to be free to lead. And Tris? Data-boy might have been building his body up, but it was all for show. He wouldn't have lasted more than a few hundred metres.

But it was annoying that he was bringing up the rear. Brice trusted Keelin to watch his back, but not Tris.

Ryann stopped every so often, holding up a hand in silence as she scanned the trees. Then she'd carry on, leading them through the undergrowth. They followed no path Brice could make out. But Ryann knew what she was doing. She was their tracker.

She stopped again, but this time she spoke.

<*Wait.*>

Then she darted forward, disappearing into the foliage. Brice looked around. Trees, undergrowth, and mud at his feet. Rain drummed down, and it seemed to free a heady, moist scent from the forest. But when Brice turned his head, he caught a meaty undertow. It seemed to be coming from Cathal. Brice wondered when he'd last brushed his teeth.

The leaves rustled, and a shape moved. Before Brice had time to react, he heard Ryann's voice, and knew she was back.

<*Possible trouble. Three warths, same ones as before.*>

<*Where?*> Keelin's voice was quiet, a whisper through the lattice.

<*A little way off. But our path brings us close.*>

<*We retreating?*> Tris sounded almost hopeful.

<*Too much doubling back. We need to move fast.*>

<*Surely it's better to be safe…*>

<*We don't have time.*> There was an urgency in her tone, harsher than normal, but it was gone when she sussed again. <*Okay. We do it like this. Move forward slowly. Keep low, don't make eye contact. No signs of aggression. If they appear and start moving towards us, we go the opposite way.*>

<*And…*>

Ryann cut Tris off. <*And we won't have a problem. Come on.*>

Brice walked in a crouch, and he felt the strain in his back. His lattice should be compensating, but maybe he was more exhausted than he felt.

It was dark under the trees, and Brice knew night had fallen. He tried to remember if warths could see in the dark.

<*One fairly close to our right. Not looking this way. Keep low.*>

Maybe it was looking for a place to bed down. But that was ridiculous—they had cubs, so they'd return to their nest.

Ryann sussed again. <*Another one, also to the right. Further back.*>

<*What about the third?*> Tris asked.

<*Not sure. Possibly behind.*>

That didn't sound good.

<*They moving or staying still?*>

<*Not sure. Confusing signals. Let me concentrate.*>

Brice followed Ryann as she turned to the left, thankfully further from the warths. At least the two she was certain of.

Then she stopped.

<*They're moving. This way.*>

<*Retreat?*> asked Tris, like he was ready to run.

<*Not yet. Wait.*> There was a pause, and then Ryann repeated herself. <*Wait.*>

Brice's mouth was dry. He wanted to tip his head back and take in some of the falling moisture. But not with Cathal's head so close. As it was, the man's short hair kept rubbing against his cheek. The stink was stronger, too, and Brice's stomach churned when he breathed it in. Maybe Cathal's wound was festering or something. Or maybe Tris had soiled himself.

But Brice knew it wasn't that. He knew it came from Cathal, and until they reached the hold-out, it would be around him constantly. He parted his lips, determined to breathe through his mouth.

<*This isn't right,*> Ryann sussed.

<*What?*> That came from both Keelin and Tris, and Brice echoed it in his mind.

<*More signals, but...confusing.*> She paused. <*Unidentified.*>

Brice focused on his heart, massaging the muscles to slow the beating. He expanded his lungs, taking in a deep pull of oxygen. His adrenaline would be pumping—even if his lattice was no longer reporting that to him—and he needed to keep it under control.

He could see the warths now, dark shapes behind the trunks, green-edged but with the orange glow of heat. At least, he thought they were warths.

<*They're slowing.*>

<*The warths, or...*> Tris didn't need to finish.

<*The warths. Maybe...*>

<*What?*>

<*Maybe they sense something.*>

<*Something?*>

<*Something not us.*>

Brice heard a click from his side, and focused on his peripheral vision. Tris had one hand raised, a lash in his grip. The hand shook, and his finger hovered over the trigger.

<*That going to do anything?*> Brice sussed. But Tris didn't answer. Maybe he didn't hear.

<*They're moving again, but slowly. We need to.... No, stay. Wait.*>

<*Wait?*> Keelin said.

<*Signals from behind.*>

<*Different? Or like…*>

<*Just different.*>

Branches shifted, and Brice knew it wasn't from the rain. In the trees level with their position, he caught more movement, higher up, like something was climbing.

A deep growl rolled through the forest, so low it seemed to come from all around. Then branches were thrown aside, and his lenses heat-signal flared brightly as a warth reared up, twice his own height. It opened its mouth with another roar, baring ugly teeth and sending spittle flying. The thing's fur was flattened by the moisture, but its skin bristled and its muscles rolled.

Then it charged.

Tris stepped forward with a yell. There was a sharp crack and Brice almost believed he saw the path of the energy bolt as it flew through the foliage. The warth stumbled, and its roar took on an angry edge. But it didn't stop.

Brice's hand found his lash, but he didn't have a chance to raise it before Tris fired again. Ryann was yelling something, but Brice couldn't make out the words over Tris' screaming.

Branches snapped. The roar grew louder. The whole forest came alive.

Then the warth flew to one side, crashing against branches and disappearing into the undergrowth.

One moment it was barrelling straight towards them, and the next it was gone.

But not because of the lash.

Brice saw it as an after-image. A shadow blurred from one side, ploughing into the beast, taking it down in a brutal tackle.

The roar rose and fell amid the sharp cracks and snaps of branches. The warth appeared again, spinning hard, limbs lashing out and teeth gnashing. Razor-sharp claws sliced through the dark, glistening with something that might not have been water. The shadow pounced again, landing on the beast's back, and Brice saw teeth in the shadow, long and sharp, and they came down on the warth's neck.

Brice's lattice let him sense this, both in real-time and in replay. The warth's roar morphed into an agonising, drawn-out cry of pain. The beast raised its great arms towards the treetop and tilted its head, snout pointing to the sky. Its fists and claws stretched back, trying to dislodge whatever clung to its back. And whatever had its neck.

A heat-intense spray of blood burst from the warth's neck, and the beast's scream became more primal. Others joined in, sharing the anguish. And the spray stopped as the shadowy creature dipped forward, its own mouth clamped over the wound. The beast's yell became almost pitiful.

Then it toppled, and the ground shook.

And for a while, nothing moved. No more shapes shifted. No more leaves rustled, and no more branches split.

<*Ryann?*> Tris' voice wavered. He crouched down again, cradling his lash. He repeated her name.

<*Wait.*>

Brice heard the sound of breathing, and only now realised how close Ryann was to him. Turning as much as he could, he saw her half-glazed eyes, and the droplet of moisture that built up then fell from the end of her nose. He saw her nostrils twitch.

<*No more movement.*>

<*What happened?*> It sounded like Keelin didn't really want to know.

<*Not sure.*>

<*The warth's still there?*>

<*Staying back.*> Leaves rustled as she turned. <*Come on.*>

<*But...*>

<*No arguing, Tris. We move.*>

And they did. As fast as they could while staying hunched over. As fast as they could to get away from whatever had just taken down the warth.

Seventeen

Brice refused to think of anything but moving. He focused on Keelin's boots, a pace in front of his own. He ignored the wet leaves that slapped his face, and the smell coming from Cathal. He pushed aside the noises of the storm and the forest and whatever followed them in the trees. And he only looked up when Ryann sussed.

<Hold-out.>

Before them stood a concrete block, slightly larger than a Proteus. But where their craft had curves and angles, the hold-out was a monolith, like someone had dumped a huge block of stone in the middle of the forest, all right-angles and coldness. There were no windows, only a dark metal door in the closest wall. It sat in a clearing, almost like the trees didn't want to come too close to something so imposing.

In that moment, Brice thought it the most wonderful thing he'd ever seen.

He turned, and saw a gap in the trees, where they arched over to form a tunnel. Beyond was another clearing, but here the ground rose in a ramp.

"Landing pad," Keelin said, her lips close to his ear, telling him what he already knew. But he basked in the warmth of her breath, and the way it blew the rain over his skin. He realised it was the first voice he'd heard, actually heard with his ears, since the cave.

<*Tris, you want to let us in?*> Ryann sussed. Tris tapped a code on the recessed panel to one side of the door. The door slid open, and when Ryann nodded again, Tris entered, followed by Keelin.

"Come on," Ryann said to Brice, her voice so low he barely caught it. And he stepped into the wonderful, cool, dry hold-out.

The door slid shut behind him, and Ryann gestured towards one of the bunks that lined the side of the room. "Let's get Cathal comfortable," she said, her voice louder this time, ringing with a slight echo.

With Keelin's help, Brice lowered Cathal onto a bunk. The mattress was clammy, with hardly any give, but just touching it made Brice realise how tired he was.

He looked around, even though he knew what to expect. Hold-outs were all the same. Opposite the five bunks were metal storage units and a work-top with a simple cooker. The table sat in the middle of the room, flanked by a couple of benches. And at the far end were two doors, one leading to the heads, and the other to the hatch. Just like the Proteus, this place had a second exit, up through the roof.

This place made the Proteus look like the height of luxury, but that was more down to how impersonal it was. The bunks held exactly the same bedding. There were extra blankets in the storage units, all of a uniform grey, the cheapest the company could find. The hold-outs were not designed to be lived in. They were a place to rest, or to hole up if a crew found themselves stranded. Like if their Proteus wasn't working properly because the company didn't care enough to make simple repairs.

Keelin made for the heads, and Tris started rummaging in one of the units, crouching and pulling boxes from drawers. Some kind of tech, Brice assumed, but it would keep him happy.

Ryann knelt by Cathal, a medi-kit open on the floor by her side. She reached over to his bandage and started to ease it off.

The smell was strong and pungent, and Ryann flinched, one hand over her mouth. But she didn't stop until the bandage was free.

Brice moved closer, peering over her shoulder. "My lenses playing up, or is that black?" he asked. Around the ragged wound the skin was discoloured, and initially Brice thought it must be blood, or maybe a bruise. But the patch looked thick, and it had spread not only down his arm but also up his neck and across his chest.

"It's black."

"That's not good, right? That's more than a simple wound."

Ryann nodded. "Far more. I need to test it." She dove into her medi-kit, pulling out a swab. She rubbed this on Cathal's wound and slotted it into the analyser. Her eyes half-closed as it fed the readings to her in, Brice assumed, a string of numbers and graphs. She sucked on her lower lip, oblivious to the rest of the room.

Brice turned to Tris. The drawer Data-boy had opened held about six items, and Brice smiled as he recognised these. Torches. Good old-fashioned flash-lights. Not much use when lenses and filters let everyone see in the dark, but Brice had used them before, training dark. Tris opened another drawer, and this one held more torches.

Did a hold-out really need so many? It annoyed Brice that the company wouldn't fix a dodgy Proteus, but they wasted money on things like this. Probably someone high up getting a kick-back, or old guidelines that had never been updated.

"Find anything good?" he asked.

"You got anything useful to do?" Tris didn't even turn his head.

"Just asking."

Tris pushed the drawer of torches closed and opened the next one down. He let out a satisfied little grunt (at least, that's what it sounded like to Brice), and reached in to pull out a small box, about the size of an outstretched hand, but about twice the thickness.

"What's that?"

"Something useful. Unlike you."

"Brice." Ryann's voice cut through the air. "I could use better lighting over here."

"No problem." She could use filters, and he knew she was trying to separate him from Tris, but he didn't step away. Not yet.

He looked at Tris, then at the storage unit. "Torch?"

"Use the bloody room system, green."

Green. Coming from Tris, that was just feeble. If it wasn't so pathetic, Brice might have been angry.

"Thanks for your help." Brice stepped away as a hand shot out. He timed it just right, and Tris' fingers only brushed the sleeve of his jacket. "I'll go do something useful. You stay here and play with yourself."

He expected retaliation for that, and was ready to respond, but Tris turned towards Ryann, his mouth open. Ryann gave him a firm look, like she was telling him off. And Tris at least had the decency to look sheepish. Brice so wanted to be in on that conversation.

The atmos controls were by the door, accessible through the usual panel. Brice placed his hand on it, and waited for the options to appear. There was a tingle in his fingers, but that was all.

"Am I doing this right?"

"Should be straightforward," Ryann said. No help there, then.

"I'll do it." Tris said. "Bloody grunt can't cope with tech."

"I'm fine," Brice said, pushing with his lattice. He wondered if lightning had hit the hold out, like it had struck the Proteus. That would be about right, the way things were going. Goddamned useless tech. They'd be better off without it.

He sussed at the panel, even though he knew that would have no effect, but the stream of curse words at least felt good. He willed his lattice to connect, imagining red lines of invisible energy flowing along his arm.

And then everything exploded in white-hot pain, and a thousand punches slammed into Brice, flinging him to the floor. Everything went dark.

His flesh burned, hot and cold at the same time, but beneath the surface. He sensed it contracting, crushing his body, and he couldn't breathe. His heart muscles hammered and then stilled, and for a moment, for the shortest of seconds, it stopped pumping.

He saw his lattice start-up levers, and they were dark and silent. A surge of power gripped him, and the levers vibrated, the movement growing in violence until they started to buckle. A couple snapped, the sound sharp and metallic, and broken handles crashed to the floor.

A blinding white light engulfed everything, flaring up with a sharp pain that remained when the darkness engulfed it.

"What the hell have you done this time, Brice?" Tris sounded angry. But Brice couldn't see him. And he sounded muffled, like he was too far away.

There were other sounds now—tapping maybe, and some muttering. Brice concentrated, and his ears popped, like he was coming out of water. The tapping was sharper, and close by. And when Tris spoke, his voice was clear.

"This thing's done for. I can reach through to the power circuits, but there's nothing to work with. Looks like our resident screw-up did it again."

"Then find a solution," Ryann said, but she sounded too far away.

Something pushed hard against the sole of Brice's left boot. "Found some rubbish. Think we should throw it out?" The pressure on his boot increased.

He might not be able to see, but at least he could feel.

Brice focused on that sensation, and he pictured where Tris must be standing. With one foot pushing his own, he must have his other one set back to keep his balance.

With a grunt, Brice kicked out, hard. His boot connected, and Tris yelled. Then something slammed into Brice's shin, and he winced at the pain. But he didn't cry out.

He willed his lattice to compensate, but it did nothing. There were no updates on damage done, no sensation of internal movement.

"You always attack people when they're down?" he said, shuffling back until he felt the wall, then pushing up it until he was sitting. He wasn't sure if he could stand, not yet. His head swam, and he felt nauseous.

"You think you deserve anything better? Bloody screw-up."

"What the hell's that supposed to mean?" Brice felt his chest rise and fall. He couldn't sense his lungs like he normally could, but he knew they were working. Just like he knew his heart was pumping blood, and his muscles were ready.

"Come on! You started all this when you fired at that warth. You're the reason we had to climb the cliff. If you hadn't been so bloody stupid, we'd never have come across that … that thing. And we'd never be in this mess. It's all your fault!"

"Yeah, like I was going to ignore a charging warth. I probably saved your life back there. Beginning to regret it now, though."

"They weren't a threat."

"No?"

"No. You made them dangerous. You're dangerous. And now…"

The next kick struck Brice's thigh, and instinctively he lashed out with an arm. It hit something solid, and he winced. He swallowed, his mouth dry now.

Tris laughed. "Thought you were good at fighting. Thought that was your speciality. No? Looks like you really are useless. Don't know why the hell you're with us anyway."

Brice pushed his back against the wall and bent his legs, bringing his feet underneath his body. The wall was cool against his hands, and he took a long breath in preparation.

"Yeah, so useless I carried Cathal the whole way here." He pushed with his legs and started to rise. "So useless I rigged the rope to get him down." The burn in his thighs lessened as his legs straightened and he stood tall. He kept his hands flat on the wall. "What the hell have you done?"

"Both of you, stop!" Keelin shouted. Brice had no idea when she'd come back from the heads. "We've got more important things to deal with."

"Like sorting out the mess this waste of space put us in."

Tris' voice was closer, almost in his face, and with a grunt Brice launched himself from the wall, pushing the nausea down as he brought his fists up. There was no finesse in the move, and he had nothing to aim at but a voice.

It was all he needed. His body followed his fists, and he felt contact as Tris cried out. Then they both fell—Brice forwards, Tris backwards. The world spun. The impact slammed through Brice, and his head hit something hard. Probably the floor.

Then there were hands clamped on his shoulders, pulling him back. He tried to stand, but the movement was too sudden. Fingers dug hard, and where they bit into his bruise from earlier a shard of pain screamed through his mind.

He rolled over and sat up. The hands still held him.

"Both of you need to stop." Keelin's voice was practically in his ear. He could feel her hair on his cheek.

"Hold him like that, and I can get a perfect shot in."

"Yeah, because you can't cope with a moving target."

"Stop!"

Brice jerked his head to one side as Ryann's voice ricocheted round the room. She said that single word loudly, and her voice was strong. But there was an edge to it, high-pitched, where it almost cracked.

Almost, but she kept it together.

"You two need to sort yourselves out, but not like this." Her words were quieter now, and she sounded tired, or maybe weary. "We work together. We're a crew. A team."

Brice opened his mouth, but caught himself in time. Saying 'he started it' probably wouldn't be the smart thing to do.

"Fine," Tris said, spitting the word out. "But I don't want anything to do with him unless I have to."

"Works for me too." Brice tried to keep his voice as civil as possible.

"Tris," Ryann said, and only now did Brice realise she wasn't sussing, but using her voice. "Any chance of getting power sorted?"

"Not likely. He wrecked it, the…."

"Enough!" She was close. Brice wondered if Ryann was holding Tris back, just as Keelin still had her hands on his shoulders. "Whatever happened, we need power. I need to do what I can for Cathal, and I'd appreciate better light."

"Torches?" Brice said. "Tris found them earlier." He said that through his teeth. It hurt to give the waste of space credit for anything.

"That'll work. Bring one over, Tris. You can sort out the power later."

Tris exhaled. “Okay.” Footsteps echoed, and a drawer opened. Then light shone, and Brice saw a beam angled to the floor. He squinted, letting his eyes grow accustomed to the light, even as it moved across to the bunks. Ryann returned to Cathal’s side, and Tris held the torch over him.

The grips on his shoulders lifted, and Brice allowed his muscles to slacken. He hadn’t realised how tightly he was holding them. Then the hands were gone, and he heard a rustle coming round from his left. When Keelin spoke, her voice was in front of him. He saw her silhouette, strands of hair hanging down, and one arm reaching out. But not quite touching.

“You dark again, Brice?”

He nodded, like he didn’t want to admit what was happening. And her hand, the one she held in front of him, wavered. She was scared. No, she was terrified.

And he understood. She might have her lattice, might even still be in contact with her baby. She might have her body warmth, and be able to communicate with the others. She might be able to pull up filters and share data. But she didn’t know what had been in the cave. She didn’t know what condition Cathal was in. She didn’t know what else was outside, waiting for them. She didn’t know if they’d be able to reach Haven.

None of them did. None of them knew a thing.

He wasn’t the only one in the dark.

EIGHTEEN

Ryann turned her back on the rest of the crew and returned to Cathal. She didn't know if that would come across as weak or strong, and to be honest she didn't care. Because she'd come too close to losing it with Tris and Brice.

Violence solved nothing. The only time Ryann inflicted harm was in training sessions, when it was expected. But when they started fighting, she'd felt her fingers roll over into a fist, and had wanted nothing more than to punch some sense into both of them.

If Keelin hadn't stepped in and pulled Brice back, Ryann knew she would have given in to that urge.

They were selfish. Or maybe self-absorbed. Tris was terrified, and was hiding behind his bravado. And Brice was struggling without his lattice. True, he was trying hard, but his surges of aggression indicated a lack of self-control.

These might be reasons, but they weren't excuses. Both of them needed to pull themselves together.

And Ryann needed to lead. She needed to set the example, and guide them. But she was failing as much as they were.

She hadn't felt this alone for a long, long time.

But she would do what she could. That was another thing she'd learnt from Cathal—you did what you could, to the best of your ability. And if you failed, then the fault was not yours to bear. The situation was whatever it was.

Cathal's condition was deteriorating. The disease—and that, she found, was the easiest way to view it—continued to take over his body. The dark patches were spreading fast. She probed them with a finger, and felt the hardness beneath the soft outer layer.

<Tris, hold the light just over his shoulder. A fraction to the left? Perfect.>

The beam wobbled, but didn't move as much as she'd feared. She'd have to remember to keep Tris more occupied in future. He avoided looking at Cathal, and she saw his nose twitch a couple of times—understandable, with the rank odour that came from Cathal's wound.

The smell worried Ryann, and it brought up memories of the time one of her father's animals had fallen, far off on the hillside. By the time they'd found the poor thing, gangrene had already set in, and there was no other option but to remove the limb—and, a few days later, put the creature down when it failed to recover.

She wouldn't be able to do that to Cathal, though. Not put him down, but amputate his arm. The wound was too deep into his shoulder. Besides, the wound itself was, strangely, clean. When she examined a sample of blood, there was little out of the ordinary, apart from a strange anti-coagulant. Whatever that was, it seemed to be working in conjunction with his own blood in stopping any infection.

She undid Cathal's shirt fully and parted the material, careful where the blood stuck it to his shoulder and chest. She lifted his body by rolling, and freed his arms. Then she folded the garment as best she could, knowing this was classic avoidance strategies, but accepting that for the moment.

Without his shirt, and with the extent of his wound clearly visible, he was no longer Cathal but a patient. She scanned him, reading the data as it scrolled across a lens. Then she zoomed in on the dark patch closest to the wound, and saw tiny hair follicles, each strand a wiry couple of millimetres. She pulled one using tweezers, and it came free easily. She placed it in a sample bag, holding her finger over the chip to label it.

Ryann used a scalpel to take a biopsy of the skin itself. She didn't dig deep, stopping before severing any blood vessels. The small sample she removed was pliable, but it contained a strength unlike normal skin. It was, in fact, closer to the leathery hide of many animals.

She placed the sample in a bag and turned to the wound itself.

The fluid that still leaked was more plasma than blood. Or maybe pus would be a better word to use. She syringed up a couple of drops, and it was translucent—cloudier than normal plasma, anyway. When she zoomed in she could make out stringy filaments, and at a guess she'd say that was to help seal the wound.

But she would also say that the sealing was happening deeper down. When she delved into his lattice—and when she could circumvent the blocks that threatened to trip her and throw her out—she saw how blood vessels in the area were closed off a short distance from the wound. It was almost as if the fluid was keeping the wound open, but stopping Cathal bleeding out.

His lattice must be involved, because there was no way that was a normal biological reaction.

She called up stronger filters, and her vision took on the fragmented, almost pixellated texture she expected. It was never ideal, but some external light would smooth the worst of the edges.

<Tris, hold the light steady over here.> The beam moved. *<Perfect. Thank you.>*

Beneath the ragged incision was a bulge, similar to an internal bleed under a blunt trauma. She brought the tip of the scalpel closer, and applied pressure. Liquid seeped around it. She pulled down, giving the liquid a run-off so that it would not distort her view. She eased the scalpel further in, until it rested on the outer layer of that bulge. She paused, taking a breath, and then pushed once more.

The pop was audible, and clear liquid arced up, jetting over Ryann's hand. It hit the glass of the torch. Tris let loose a yell, and the beam jerked away.

<Tris! Hold it steady!>

<Sorry,> he sussed, privately.

Tris didn't have her training, and so she shouldn't be shocked that he'd reacted as he did. He was young. She couldn't be annoyed at him.

<*Understandable reaction. This is tough on all of us. You're doing great.*> She wondered if that might come across as patronising, but she saw him nod, and knew he accepted her words.

He brought the beam back down. The light was different, the waveforms clashing with her filters, and she considered asking Tris to wipe the glass. But that would only remind him of what had just happened. She'd finish her examination first.

<*Down a fraction more, Tris, please.*>

The light dropped. And Cathal's boot thudded against the wall.

Ryann didn't see the movement, but what else could have made that sound?

And then his whole body spasmed. His arms and legs twitched, and the boot kicked the wall again and again. A hand slapped against Ryann's thigh. She pulled the scalpel from his wound, heard it hit the floor, and placed a hand on his vibrating, lurching chest.

His skin rippled, pushing against her palm. And at the edge of the wound, bulges formed and receded, like bubbles.

Cathal threw his head back, foam creeping to the corners of his mouth. His teeth grinded, but that didn't disguise the keening whine that seeped from his mouth.

Brice cursed loudly, and he was by Cathal's feet, reaching down to pin them to the bunk, struggling as they lashed out at him. He swore, then threw his own weight across them, like he had in the cave.

Tris yelled, and the torch clattered to the floor, the light rolling around. It sprayed the wall with dancing shadows.

And Cathal's convulsions stopped. The rippling of his skin abated, and the pustules in his shoulder faded into the surrounding tissue. His head stilled, only the fine sheen of sweat on his forehead a reminder of his exertions.

"What's happening?" Keelin spoke, her voice small and cracked, and simultaneously Ryann heard her inner thoughts, bursting out uncontrollably.

<That's good, right? If he moves, he's still alive. That might mean he's coming round. He's going to be okay. We're going to get out of this, aren't we? Are we?>

<Keelin, it's fine. We're all fine.>

But Ryann wasn't sure she believed that.

Brice eased himself off Cathal's legs. He smoothed the man's trousers, and straightened one boot.

The rolling torch came to a rest, casting its beam into a corner, where two concrete walls met. Ryann followed them round, to the other corners, and then to the solid roof over their heads. Cold and unmoving, Ryann thought, and devoid of life.

NINETEEN

"What just happened?" Brice asked. He knew this echoed Keelin's question, but he needed an answer.

Ryann shook her head, as if that told him anything. She reached for a fresh dressing and sealed it over Cathal's shoulder. Then she picked up his shirt.

"Keelin, a bit of help?" she said.

Brice watched them pull Cathal up and work his arms into his shirt-sleeves. Then they lay him back down and fastened the buttons right up to his neck. Ryann smoothed the material over his chest, and rested his arms by his side.

He looked like he was sleeping. If you ignored the blackness creeping up his neck, and the smell.

Only then did Ryann look at Brice. Her face was lined and pale. Maybe it was the effect of the light from the torch, and the shadows it cast, but Brice had never seen her looking so old.

"Okay," she said, putting her hands on her hips, kind of like Cathal would sometimes do. "Our situation. We're safe. That's important. But we have problems."

Maybe Tris sussed something, because she shot him a look before continuing.

"A summary. One, Cathal is sick. I've done what little I can, but he needs Haven's experts. Two, the hold-out's power is compromised. Tris, your thoughts please."

Brice expected insults, but Ryann glared at the techie, and he spoke in a quiet, slow voice. "Power's very limited. Far as I can tell, we're running on auxiliary, but it's locking me out of most of the systems."

"Just so we all know where we stand, how long does auxiliary last?"

Tris shrugged. "Maybe twelve hours."

"Okay. Third problem. Contact. Keelin, how's our Proteus?"

"Still down." Her mouth opened, like she wanted to say more, but her eyes dropped and her head shook.

"And I take it we can't reach Haven."

She didn't phrase that as a question, but Tris answered anyway. "Not in this storm. And not since someone screwed the power."

Ryann's hand shot up, and she gave him another look.

"But we still have twelve hours of power, right?" Brice said, thinking how twelve hours would take them through the night. Things always looked better in daylight. "And even without power, we can cope. Aren't the hold-out's supposed to be fully equipped?"

Ryann nodded. "Enough to survive for a week. But the lack of power limits us. No power, no atmos control. These buildings are designed to be air-tight. We do have the emergency hatch, but that brings us on to our fourth problem." Ryan paused. "We open that to let air in, but what else comes in?"

Brice swallowed dryly. He didn't want to answer that question.

"So this is what we do," Ryann continued, putting her hands on her hips. "Power's priority, so Tris, see what you can do. Keelin, you help. Brice," and here she nodded towards the storage units, "give us a full inventory." Then she turned to the rear of the hold out. "I'll recon outside."

"No!" Keelin said, the word sharp, tumbling out like she couldn't stop it. "I mean, you…we don't know what's out there. What if…"

Ryann held up a hand, and Keelin trailed off.

"We need to know the situation. Without power, we have no external sensors. And I'm the tracker. If I sense anything, I won't even open the hatch. And if it's safe, I'll only take a quick look anyway. Believe me, I don't want to go out there unless I have to."

"But if we get the power back on, we'll have sensors. We don't need to rush."

Ryann glanced at Cathal. Brice wasn't sure if anyone else caught the movement.

"We don't know how long that will take. We need maximum data in minimum time. We work round any problems. It's what we do." She hesitated, then stepped towards the rear door. "Let's do this." The words sounded like an echo of Cathal. And like an echo, they had no substance of their own.

The door shut behind her, and Brice turned to the storage units.

The torch Tris had dropped was still the only source of light in the room, so Brice first opened the drawer with the torches and pulled out another one. He turned it on, running through the settings. He couldn't understand why they made these things so complicated. He could change the angle and intensity of the beam, and even the make-up of the light itself. There were coloured filters, but also different wavelength settings. One was even supposed to mimic night-vision, which seemed particularly useless—surely having a light source did away with the need for night vision?

Brice selected a bright beam with a harsh blue hue, which he knew would hurt his eyes after a while, but it did a great job of banishing the shadows wherever he pointed it. Far better than the yellow glow from the torch Tris had been using, before he let it fall like a frightened child.

He didn't even use the wrist-strap. Brice wondered how Datamonkey even got through basic training.

Tris was by the door. He'd removed the wall panel around the controls, and was prodding around inside. Keelin stood, practically touching him, and every now and then she'd bring a hand up and point.

Techies and pilots always stuck together. Brice had noticed that back in training, even before the final lattice tweaks, when specialities were still supposed to be wide open. It was like they had their own language, like they couldn't use normal words for stuff. Keelin and Tris would be using this technobabble now, sussing back and forth. It wasn't like they even needed to suss, though. Brice wouldn't understand a word of it.

He turned back to the stores. He had his own job to do, even if it was the kind of thing anyone could do. But it was grunt-work. It was a job to keep the greenest of the green out of the way.

Ryann was as bad as Cathal. No, worse. She wavered too much. She didn't have Cathal's solidity.

But, technically, she was in charge. He had to follow her orders, as pathetic as they were.

What else could he do?

The supplies in the hold-out were predictable enough that Brice could keep a list in his head, even without access to data banks. He found toolkits, a step up from basic but nothing special. Another drawer held five lashes, with double-strength power-packs. Below this were knives, each one in a separate sheath, and also sealed in clear plastic. It looked like they'd never been touched.

He carried on. Medical supplies, a few hygiene items, spare clothing and blankets. Everything was a bland grey colour, all standard issue. The blankets reminded Brice of Cathal's quarters back on the Proteus. Serviceable was the word that came to mind. This stuff, all the supplies—they'd do the job, but they were nothing to get excited about.

Even the food was bland. Brice ran a finger across the rows of foodpacks, reading the labels. Each one had a name, then nutritional information. Ingredients came last, because they were not important. Who cared what it tasted like, as long as it supplied the required amount of energy or whatever?

But there was an allergy warning, as ridiculous as that was. When was the last time anyone had an allergic reaction to food? The body's lattice would compensate. It could isolate toxins and ejected them from the body. The need to put such pointless information on a foodpack made Brice laugh out loud.

"You playing about over there, or doing something useful?"

Brice brought the torch up, shining it straight at Tris. The data-freak cursed, and shielded his eyes. Keelin put a hand on his shoulder and dipped her head. Brice lowered the beam.

"You fixed the power yet?" he said, trying to keep his tone light because he knew this would wind Tris up.

"Not after the way you screwed it."

"Better get back to work then."

"You think you can do any better?"

Brice wanted to come back with something strong, but he knew Tris had him there. And the moron's supercilious grin just added to his frustrations. He thought of ploughing a fist into that smug face. He imagined the baby crying out as he staggered back. There wouldn't even have to be any blood, and Tris would be beaten. He was pathetic.

Keelin's other hand came round, so she had one on each of Tris' shoulders, and she moved her face in front of his. She didn't speak, but Brice knew she was sussing. Tris looked at her, glared back at Brice, and then nodded. His stance softened, and he snorted before turning back to the wires behind the door controls.

Keelin turned to Brice, shaking her head. He tried to read her expression, but hair hung over her eyes as usual. She didn't smile. And then she, too, turned her back on Brice.

He looked at the foodpack in his hand, and the allergy warning wasn't so funny now.

Tris and Keelin sussed privately, cutting Brice out and leaving him on his own. His muscles ached, because his lattice was doing nothing to aid recovery. He felt cold, his clothing held too much water, and the grit and silt and whatever else irritated his skin. He was the grunt, but without his lattice he was even less.

And without his lattice, he had no protection.

The foodpack in his hand was a curry, and it listed nuts as a possible risk. Was Brice allergic to them? He had no idea.

He pictured the scene—a meal in the semi-dark, and Brice convulsing as the nut paste or whatever it was attacked his body. He imagined the others rushing to his aid as he collapsed on the floor, shaking as violently as Cathal had done. He imagined how he'd go into a coma. Maybe Ryann would have to shove something into his mouth to keep his airway open, or stop his throat swelling and blocking.

Maybe she'd be too late.

But even if she was in time, his chances of survival were low.

Two unconscious crew-members. If the remaining three couldn't carry them both, they'd have to make a decision—the commander or the grunt.

Brice had no doubt which way they'd go.

He wondered if Ryann would give him something to end it, or if they'd leave him in the hold-out. Maybe they'd send someone out to retrieve his body once they were safely in Haven.

And would anyone care? Ryann might act upset, but that would be because she couldn't keep her crew together. Tris would probably be pleased. And Keelin?

If Brice thought she cared, he knew he was kidding himself. She was too close to Tris, too wrapped up in their techno-crap.

Brice was nothing.

TWENTY

Ryann had to get out.

Was that selfish? She wasn't sure. All she knew for certain was that the walls were closing in, and that she couldn't think. She needed space. She needed to get out of that tomb.

She was failing. She had no idea how to prevent Cathal's condition from deteriorating. Without power, she had no way of calling for help. And she could do nothing to stop the animosity between Brice and Tris.

Her crew was falling apart. And all she wanted to do was run away.

In the space behind the door, she took a long, deep breath. The air was close and still, almost stale, but above her was the hatch. Maybe a lungful of the night air would help. Maybe the rain on her face would wake her up.

She climbed the metal rungs, noticing how polished they were. She didn't know if that was because they hadn't been used, or because this hold-out had been tended recently. With the lack of power, there was no way of accessing the building's data.

Ryann reached the hatch, and she paused, pushing out with her lattice, reaching through the thick concrete and the harsh metal. Beyond the hold-out, the signals were fluid, more animated, and she searched for familiar traces.

There were no warths but there was something else.

She closed her eyes and focused. The trace was strong but indistinct, and that indicated a number of beings at a distance. So there was more than one of those creatures. Ryann concentrated, but she couldn't get a firm grasp. She had no idea how many there were.

But none of the creatures were close to the hatch. There was no risk. She had to do this.

Ryann spun the rotary plate on the hatch. Then she clicked the clasp open and pushed.

Water ran down the walls before she'd pushed the hatch fully open, and the roar of the storm washed over her. Rain stung her face, and the sky lit up as a peal of thunder followed the lightning. Treetops whipped back and forth, the rustling of the leaves angry and agitated.

And Ryann welcomed it all.

She pulled up filters to combat the darkness, and checked the traces again. The creatures were still at a distance, but they seemed…interested. She imagined they must have noticed the hatch opening.

Ryann climbed a rung higher, and her head cleared the hatch. Water splashed on the concrete roof, pooling in places so that it looked almost alive. She looked to the edges of the hold-out, and out into the trees. There was too much movement, but she could sense patches of stillness, like the void that surrounded the creature in the cave.

Ryann realised she'd felt that in the hold-out, too. Not from the forest, but from Cathal. His lattice fought hard, but beneath the heat and energy was a similar dark limbo.

She knew what that had to mean, and it terrified her.

She steadied her feet and turned, making a full three-sixty. She scanned, reading the forest to the best of her abilities. She'd told Keelin they needed data, and so she pulled as much in as possible. She mapped the trees, and the landing pad. Further out were paths, and Ryann caught the traces of warths, maybe a few days old.

But they were not as strong as the signals from the creatures that surrounded the hold-out.

They evaded her sight, but she knew they were there. They hid in the shadows, at ground level and higher up. She could not detect individuals, but felt them like a being with many parts, like a connected pack.

A multitude, with a single purpose.

She pushed further, seeking a stronger signal, something that would indicate a leader, or maybe a consciousness driving the rest. But she found nothing.

They were an army without a head.

They watched, and they waited.

Ryann shuddered with cold realisation.

There was no help coming from Haven. Tris would not get power restored—asking him to look into it had only been a diversion. Keelin had no way of pulling the Proteus from the river. If they left the hold-out, they would be at the mercy of the swarm of creatures. And if they stayed, Cathal's condition would become even more serious.

Ryann climbed down and sealed the hatch. The clank echoed heavily, and the water on the rungs chilled her hands. She splashed to the floor, and rested one hand on the door.

They were lost. Whatever happened, things could only get worse.

The crew were relying on her. She had to lead them. But there was nothing she could do beyond offer some kind of reassurance. And even that would be wrong. She couldn't lie to them.

She thought of her father's wounded livestock, the ones he put out of their misery before their suffering became intolerable. And Ryann knew she had the means to do that. She knew how to over-administer drugs. She knew how to stop the flow of blood to the brain in a number of relatively painless ways.

But she couldn't do that. Not to herself, and not to the crew. If there was any hope, no matter how small, she couldn't contemplate something so drastic.

She wasn't cut out to be a leader. She was a second—care for the crew, and leave the hard decisions up to someone else. Someone more experienced, someone with a better mind. But there was nobody like that. With Cathal indisposed, she was on her own.

What would Cathal do?

Ryann pictured him, back on the Proteus, when they lay under the water. She saw him in the cave, after they'd climbed to escape from the warths. And she knew what he'd do.

He'd do what he did in any situation. He'd call for suggestions. He'd gather information. He'd listen and analyse.

Ryann nodded. She could do that.

She pushed the door open and returned to her crew.

TWENTY-ONE

"But we're safe, right?" Tris said. "They can't get in. Tell me we're safe."

"We're as safe as we can be," Ryann said, keeping her voice steady. She'd informed them of the creatures, telling herself she wasn't going to sugar-coat any of this. They deserved the truth.

"Not even a warth could break through that door," Keelin said, almost to herself.

"One of those things took down a warth."

"A warth isn't a thick layer of metal. Or a solid reinforced concrete wall." Keelin turned to Tris now, "Even a lash can knock a warth down if you get the right angle."

"So nothing's invulnerable."

"Ryann said we're as safe as we can be." Keelin's voice was soft and steady, but Ryann detected a slight hesitation. "These buildings were built to survive."

"But…but you've seen what those things can do. They took Cathal down in an instant. They bit him, Keelin! They bit him and left him for dead. What happens when they break in here? We don't stand a chance! We might as well give up."

Ryann never saw the slap coming, and nor did Tris. His head jerked to one side as the sharp sound echoed around the room, leaving a harsh stillness in its wake.

Tris rubbed his cheek, then examined his palm, as if he expected to see blood. His mouth hung open.

Ryann knew she should step in. She should have read the signs and acted sooner. She was failing once more.

"We don't know what's going to happen," Keelin said, her voice barely audible. She stretched her fingers. Ryann knew her hand must be smarting. "But we're as safe as we can be for the moment. Panic isn't going to help. We need to stay calm"

"Keelin's right," Ryann said, stepping in before Keelin's nerves overwhelmed the girl. "I don't like this situation any more than you do, but we make the best of it. We think clearly, and we stay calm." That was obvious, and Tris knew it. There was no reason for Ryann to mention it. Cathal would not waste words like this. "So, our strategy. Ideas. Comments."

Stillness descended again. Ryann knew how close she was to shaking, and she took a deep breath. She pulled the adrenaline in, and steadied her body and mind. And her voice.

"How is he?" Brice asked, nodding to the bunk. He didn't meet her eyes.

"I've done everything I can."

"So we have to get him back to Haven."

"Yes."

"But we don't have power to call them up."

"No." Let Brice make his summary, she thought. It might clear the minds of the others, at least enough for fresh ideas to surface.

"But we have other equipment. There's stuff in the stores I don't know about. Not my speciality."

Ryann saw his glance towards Tris, and there was a flicker of anger, but he pushed it down. She jumped in before it could reappear.

"Tris, that's your area. We likely to have anything that could help?"

His mouth opened and closed a few times, and his hand returned to rub the redness on his cheek.

"You found something earlier?" Ryann needed to drag him from his funk. "When we first came in, you were rooting around, right?"

He shrugged, and his eyes darted to the storage units. "Saw a few relays before, but they're not going to push through the concrete. Not all the way to Haven."

"So we need to get out?" Brice said.

Tris snorted, and Ryann held up a hand as fast as she could. She didn't need this descending into another fight.

"Tris, let's talk this through," she said. "We'll explore ideas, regardless of practicalities. At the moment."

He huffed. "Fine. Yes, if we got out, we might be able to reach Haven. But it depends on how much we have, where we are, the storm…there are too many variables."

"Okay. Let's cut out one of them at least. Take a look at what we've got."

Tris took the few steps to the storage unit. Brice opened his mouth, then closed it. Probably a wise move, whatever he was going to say.

<*Talk to me,*> she sussed to Keelin, who stood to one side, watching both Tris and Brice. <*Tell me again how you're doing.*>

<*Don't know.*>

<*Feel the Proteus still?*>

<*She's too weak. She doesn't want to be disturbed. I need to…I need to let her rest.*>

<*Sometimes that's all we can do. If you can continue to monitor her, that's something.*> And it would give Keelin a focus.

Tris was pulling equipment from different drawers, stacking objects neatly in two piles. Ryann recognised most of the stuff, but this was Tris' area of expertise. She needed to give him ownership.

"What do we have, Tris?"

"Nothing special, just a few boosters, bits and pieces. A couple of old relays, even an X-43. There's some extra power packs, too, but they're the Sorin ones, and they've leaked. Most sitting somewhere between sixty and seventy percent total."

"Is that enough to reach Haven?"

"Not from in here."

"What about outside?" She saw his head snap round, and added quickly, "Just so we know where we stand."

He nodded. "Okay. If this stuff was in the open, yes. It could reach Haven, but that depends on other things…"

"Like the storm. I get that. Anything else affect it?"

He shrugged. "Geography. The higher up we are, the straighter the signal path, and the less power we need. Basic physics."

If there was some kind of rebuke in that statement, Ryann let it go. She called up a map of the area, scanned until she found what she needed. "And we're in a dip here." She pushed the information to Tris. "You seeing this?"

"Analysing data."

Ryann wanted to smile when he said that. It might have been a cold statement, but it told her that he was pushing emotions to one side. He was starting to think logically.

"We're too low. The power-packs we have wouldn't be enough."

"What about the landing pad?" Brice said.

Tris glared at him. "That's the same altitude, idiot."

Ryann held up both hands, palms out. "Keep it civil. We listen to any suggestions, remember?"

Tris huffed, but turned away from Brice. Strangely, Brice hadn't reacted. His head stayed down, and his shoulders remained slumped. And now that Ryann thought of it, his voice had been dispassionate. Although he asked a question, there was no lift at the end. It was as if he'd already given up.

Ryann didn't think that was a good sign at all.

"There's another landing pad, though," Keelin said. "About a half-k away. It's higher."

"Show us," Ryann said, before anyone could knock this back.

A new map blinked into existence on her lens, a warm glow at their current location. Further out—but zooming in as she shifted her focus—was a landing pad on a rise, almost a hill.

"You got this, Tris?" she asked. "Brice?"

And that was a mistake. Brice clenched his jaw, and she saw his chest rise high as he took a deep breath.

<*You didn't get it,*> she sussed to him, privately. It wasn't a question. She needed him to understand that she knew.

He didn't respond.

<*And you can't hear this, can you?*>

Of course there was no response. Something else to deal with.

"How long to get there?" she asked, focusing on the more immediate issue.

"Ten minutes," Tris said.

"Could do a half-k in five, easily," Brice muttered. Tris rounded on him, but Brice shrugged. "Just saying. Suppose the storm and stuff might slow me down."

Ryann should have been pleased that Brice avoided a confrontation, but it made him appear weak. Tris seemed to sense this, too, because his sneer turned into a dismissive snort, and he looked down at the piles of equipment, then back to Ryann.

"Wouldn't make a difference how fast we moved," he said. "Those things out there would be on us the moment we stepped out."

And that stopped the conversation. It was all theory, all 'what-if's. None of it would work while the army of monsters surrounded them. All the talk of raising Haven was just that—talk and nothing more.

And even if Haven sent out a search party, they'd target the Proteus. They'd go to the Tumbler. Maybe they'd track the crew, but what would happen when they came across the creatures?

At least the hold-out gave them some protection.

Even a tomb slowed decomposition.

The sound of footsteps echoed off the cold walls, and Ryann look up. Brice walked towards the rear door.

"I need to see," he said, without turning.

Keelin moved towards him, and grabbed his shoulder. "Ryann's already looked," she said.

"I know."

"But she can…she's more suited to observation."

"I can see."

"It's dark out there."

He held up a torch. Then he took another step, and placed a hand on the door.

"You don't need to look, Brice," Ryann said, keeping her tones soft.

He nodded, but said "I think I do. Just to…just for myself. To clarify, you know?"

There was more to it, but Brice wasn't willing to explain. Maybe he didn't fully understand himself. Maybe he needed a moment of escape, like Ryann had done, earlier.

"Those things are out there," Keelin said.

"But at a distance. Right, Ryann?"

"They were when I looked."

"But what if they've moved? What if they're already on the roof?" Keelin shuddered as she spoke. "What if they attack the moment you open the hatch?"

Brice didn't answer. His arm flexed as he prepared to push the door. Ryann knew he was determined. Standing in his way would only cause more conflict.

"I'll come to the bottom of the ladder," she said, the decision coming fast. "I sense them close, I let you know, and you don't open the hatch. Okay?"

He hesitated, then nodded. She didn't like that hesitation.

"You go against this, and I'll be back through that door and leave you to them." The threat sounded weak. "No risks, Brice. I won't put the others in danger because of this. I say it's clear, you open the hatch and take a look. Otherwise, the hatch stays sealed. Clear?"

He swallowed, then nodded. "I need to see," he repeated, and Ryann knew he'd open that hatch regardless.

TWENTY-TWO

The metal rungs chilled Brice's fingers, and that pushed him to keep climbing. Light came from below, where Ryann held her torch steady. He hadn't turned his on yet. He let the shadows reach out to him. They were nothing to fear. He was dark anyway.

He reached the hatch, and glanced down to Ryann. Her features were masked by the light, but he thought he saw her head nod.

"Go on," she said.

He spun the rotary plate, then flicked the catch and pushed. Chilled air rushed in, bringing a spray of moisture that grew into a downpour, and by the time the hatch was fully open his face was drenched. The rain ran down his head and neck, sliding under his jacket.

That almost made him feel alive.

Above him, the sky was rolling blackness. There was a moon somewhere, and stars, maybe even Metis, but all was obscured by the clouds and the storm.

Brice gripped the torch, his thumb nudging the controls to set a wide beam. And then he climbed up higher.

The rain stung him from the sides now, and water splashed back from the roof of the hold-out.

He brought the torch round in a slow arc, the beam angled along the flat concrete surface and into the surrounding forest. Water splashed up, forming a fine mist, behind which the wind threw the trees about angrily. He imagined they were trying to escape, but were trapped by their roots and trunks. He imagined them tearing loose, a great rip as they experienced a moment of freedom before crashing to the ground, their life support system in tatters. But they'd have that one beautiful moment before they died.

Brice climbed onto the roof.

Ryann might have said something, but he ignored her. This was what he needed—to be free of the hold-out, to be in the open. There was nothing for him back below. He was no longer a part of the crew. Nothing but a grunt, a waste of space with no skills.

But out here, he was alive. The wind pulled at him, and the rain pounded down, and he had never felt so invigorated. This might be his final moment, but he was going to savour it.

He turned slowly, playing the torch into the trees. The creatures were out there, and they would see him. They must know he was unprotected. The lash in its holster would do nothing, and he wasn't going anywhere near his knives. And the creatures could jump. From the closest trees, they could reach the concrete roof with ease. If they wanted him, they could take him.

Maybe that was what he wanted.

And he could see them now, dark shapes within the branches. Amongst the constant violent motion of the trees, they were immovable shadows, watching and waiting.

Brice turned, full circle. Patches of dark solidity dotted the forest.

Some held out long arms, and claws glinted as the torch-light struck them. Their torsos were small but muscular, and their skin looked dark and leathery, matching what he'd felt back in the caves.

The creatures didn't flinch as water ran down their hairless heads. Their eyes were large pits, black but with cloud-like swirls. The rain washed over these orbs, giving them a glassy sheen, before carrying on, round the two holes where a nose should be, and on to their mouths. Some were open, revealing sharp, pointed teeth, fang-like and yellow.

And Brice could smell them now. Above the fragrance of the forest, and over the stink of mud, was the stench of decay. It had a meaty, coppery tone that made his stomach churn.

But it was the same stench that came from Cathal, and the same stench that was slowly filling the hold-out. At least out here, there was fresh rain. At least there was that fleeting moment of life.

Brice continued to scan, and brought his torch round to the tunnel of trees that led to the landing pad. Creatures hid in the trees, and Brice saw one shift. It seemed to pull back, and then it was gone. He saw the movement as an after-image, a streak of darkness that flew from one tree to the next.

A creature had jumped onto Cathal. Another had taken out a warth.

And that must have been when his thumb twitched, because the light changed quality, taking on a blue tinge. The creatures' hides glistened, water on leather appearing as armour, and the claws as the deadly weapons they were.

In that instance, Brice didn't want to die.

He stepped back, towards the hatch, only now aware of how close to the edge of the roof he was. In the distance he heard Ryann calling.

His hand shook. He didn't want one of those things ripping into his neck, or slashing at him with its claws. He was stupid to be up here, on his own, with no protection.

The torch beam changed again, this time sending out a reddish hue that turned the trees to blood and made him cry out. The crimson darkness rippled with countless bodies as limbs flexed, ready to tear him to pieces.

And suddenly he remembered Cathal's fit. He remembered the way the man's whole body had jerked about uncontrollably, like a fish out of water. No, like a test subject being shocked repeatedly.

That seemed to happen suddenly, but nothing was without reason. Something had triggered that reaction.

With purpose, Brice thumbed the torch control panel. Without his lattice he couldn't read the settings, but he knew how to manually change them.

The beam grew brilliantly white, and teeth glowed, and eyes hung in the trees like luminous balls.

Brice thumbed the next setting, and the light took on a yellow hue, not as intense as before. It was almost comforting.

This time the forest writhed.

When the light hit the creatures, they shuddered, retreating deeper into the foliage, hiding behind branches and leaves. A sibilance cut though the pounding of the rain and the rumbling of the thunder, like an angry, pained hiss.

He turned a full circle, and all the creatures pushed to escape the light. When he returned to where he started, they reacted with more venom, baring their fangs as they backed off, some bringing their arms round to protect themselves. Their hides rippled in the torchlight.

Brice saw his own breath in front of his face, a haze that drifted off as the beam moved.

A peal of thunder washed through the forest, and the lightning lit the sky with an orange glow. There was no forking, just a flash, as if someone had found a light-switch for the clouds and had flicked it a couple of times. Brice instinctively flinched.

But the creatures didn't seem bothered. They were more concerned with the light from his torch.

That was important. Again, he remembered Cathal spasming in the light. And now, he didn't want to be out here anymore.

"Brice?" Ryann's voice came up from the hatch, just by his feet now. He looked down. She had one hand on a rung, as if she were about to climb up, and one knee was raised.

"Coming down," he said, then took one final look around the trees, bathing them with the light that seemed to send the creatures scurrying away.

"They're angry." Ryann's voice was barely audible. "And … something else."

Brice nodded, but didn't know if she saw the movement. Thoughts raced through his head as he spun the rotary plate to seal the hatch.

"What happened to them?" she asked when he drew level with her. But he held up a hand. Before he said anything, he needed to be sure.

He ignored Tris' comment and Keelin's look when he entered the main room. He stepped across to the bunks.

With the blanket covering his body, Cathal looked like he was deep in peaceful sleep. For a fleeting moment Brice wanted to swap places. He wanted to be laid out, unconcerned with the world outside, blissful in ignorance. He wanted nothing more than to close his eyes and make this all disappear.

But he stepped closer, breathing through his mouth in anticipation of the stench. He couldn't be distracted. He kept the torch beam angled to the floor, the yellow light following his footsteps. A flick of his thumb focused the beam, and then he raised it. The beam crawled across the floor and up the side of the bunk.

As it reached Cathal's head, the man moved. His eyes remained closed, but they flickered. His head twisted violently to one side, and spittle flew from his mouth.

Brice moved the beam away quickly, up to the wall. If he was going to check this out, he needed to do it properly.

Brice pulled back the blanket and unbuttoned Cathal's shirt with one hand. He gagged at the stench, and looked down at the worryingly familiar black covering that reached almost across Cathal's chest now. He thought of what he'd seen hiding in the trees.

"What are you doing, Brice?" Ryann was by his shoulder, but she wasn't trying to stop him.

"Not sure," he said, and it was only partly a lie.

He brought the beam round on the wall, and then lowered the yellow glow onto Cathal's chest.

And this time, there was no surprise when Cathal started to thrash about.

TWENTY-THREE

Somehow, Ryann knew what was about to happen. It made sense, like the pieces of a puzzle falling into place.

Cathal spasmed. Where the light fell on him, his skin rippled. The darker, leathery patches stretched and bulged, and a fine mist rose, like sweat evaporating. But it carried the stench of his wound with it, rancid and pungent.

An arm shot out, striking her leg before flailing in the air. Cathal moaned, and there was a low hiss at the back of his throat that grew into an angry rattle.

His body buckled, his back rising from the bunk. His other hand smacked against the wall with a crunch. The hiss grew into a cry of pain. Through her connection, Ryann felt his lattice flare bright, burning up, and a thousand synapses sparked.

"Enough!"

Brice looked at her, then back at Cathal, his mouth open, like he only now realised what he was doing. The beam jerked to the floor, illuminating the pool of water by his feet. And Cathal grew still once more.

"Tell me."

She sensed Tris and Keelin, her hand on his shoulder, and his fist clenched. She considered sussing, but she needed to concentrate on what Brice had to say. They all did.

Brice didn't meet her eyes when he spoke, and his voice was quiet but steady. She heard each breath he took.

"Outside," he started, "I changed the light setting. Something startled me, and my finger slipped. I started running through all the settings, just to see what happened. Then I got to one setting, and those things…reacted. It was like they were hiding from the light, like they were scared of it. And then…well, I needed to be sure. I wasn't trying to hurt him."

Ryann never thought he was. But Brice wasn't saying that for her benefit, was he?

"And Cathal reacted in the same manner as the creatures outside?"

He shook his head. "They hid from the light."

"Which setting."

Brice held the torch out to her. "I can't read it. The setting it's on now."

Ryann held a finger over the control, and pulled the data up. Intensity, luminosity, angle, remaining power, streams of other figures. But in large letters, displayed in the most prominent data field in her lens, was the name for that setting.

"Sol," she said.

"They're scared of daylight?" Tris' tone suggested confusion but also disbelief, and Ryann knew he wasn't alone in that. Sol was, indeed, the closest artificial simulation of sunlight. It was what they used in communal areas in Haven, replenishing vitamin D and keeping them healthy. It was the basis of the light in the greenhouses. It was vital for life, and yet these creatures shunned it. And, if Cathal's reaction was any indication, with good reason.

"Or something in its make-up. Might be a particular wavelength. We can't know for sure."

"That's why they live in caves," Keelin said. "That's why we've never seen them before."

Ryann nodded. It was a decent enough working hypothesis. But where the creatures came from wasn't a priority at the moment.

Brice buttoned up Cathal's shirt, then covered him with the blanket. He paused, then pulled it up, over his head. No part of his skin, either normal or leathery, was visible.

Then Brice reached for the torch. Ryann passed it over, intrigued where he was going with this. He turned the torch over in his hands a few times, then pulled at the sleeve near the glass. It slid down, and the torch became a lantern, spreading light in all directions.

He placed it carefully on the floor, watching Cathal. Ryann saw no movement.

“If they stay away from this sol setting, we’re safe,” he said, choosing his words with care. “We keep Cathal covered.”

It made sense, but Ryann didn’t like not seeing Cathal. It seemed too final, like a reminder of what would—could—eventually happen. And he was still changing, even if he was hidden from view.

“But we need to get out,” she said, and there was a murmur of assent from both Keelin and Tris. “We need to call Haven.”

“Maybe we can.”

Tris huffed, but Ryann raised a hand. “Go on,” she said to Brice. “Work through it.”

She didn’t allow hope to rise. Not yet. But she felt a surge of something like pride. Brice had the start of an idea, and even if it turned out to be impractical, it might trigger more ideas. And Tris was staying calm. That would be Keelin’s influence, true, but it meant they were calm enough to work together. Like a team. Like a crew.

And maybe this was how they would survive—not through a leader telling them what to do, but through working together.

“The other landing pad’s a half-k away, right? And we have relays and boosters, and whatever else we need.” He waved a hand at the lantern. “And now we have something that keeps the creatures away.”

“It’ll never work,” Tris said, but it wasn’t an accusation or a threat. His words came from doubt and fear.

“Maybe not,” Ryann said. “But don’t give up too easily. Brice, carry on.”

He nodded. “Tris, what equipment would we need to reach Haven from that landing pad?”

Tris seemed about to make some comment, but he bit his lip, and closed his eyes. “Relay, and maybe ten boosters.”

"Then what? They pick up a message straight away?"

"Possibly. Might get an instant response."

"But might take time."

"And if you think I'm staying outside, with those things around, you're out of your head."

Brice nodded. "Fair enough." He smiled. "Maybe I am." But he said that too quietly for it to be in jest.

"We have enough equipment in here, Tris?" she asked, giving Brice time to collect his thoughts and focus his mind.

"Sure. More than enough. Just don't see how practical it would be, though. Even if we set up a system, we'd have to monitor it. Too much trouble to go to just to send off a random message and hope it hits home."

"But we can monitor remotely." Ryann might not have his tech training, but she had some understanding of how these things worked.

"Without power, can't monitor from inside the hold-out. Concrete's treated."

"But can we set up a closer boost?"

"Give me a moment." Tris turned to the storage units and opened drawers. Meanwhile, Brice bent down to study the torch/lattice. His shadow loomed large on the wall, hovering over Cathal.

"Brice?" Ryann said, and he looked up.

"Just a thought. If we leave stuff out in the open, it's vulnerable. We need to protect it."

She looked to the torch, understanding. "Leave a torch with the equipment, and the creatures don't come near." She gave Brice a smile. "Good thinking."

"We'd need a second one, on our roof." This came from Tris. He held a couple of boosters in his hands, and his shadow stretched out onto the open stores.

"What have you worked out?"

"Still don't think much of our chances out there, so this is theoretical only. Main group of boosters and a relay at the pad. Then we put another relay and booster on the roof of this hold-out, with another lantern. A third relay in here, and we'd be able to talk to Haven without going out there."

"Delayed signal, or instant communication?" Ryann liked where this was going.

"Pretty much instant. Storm might introduce a short delay, but nothing more than a couple of seconds." Tris smiled.

"But we still need someone to set up the stuff outside," Keelin said.

Tris' face fell. "Like I said, it's only theoretical. Yes, someone would have to go out there. And get ripped to shreds by those things."

"Unless we used torches," Brice said, nudging the lantern with his foot. The shadows on the walls jerked, and Keelin flinched away from them.

Tris laughed. "What, we go out there waving torches around, and hope that works?"

"Better than waving lashes around. At least we know the torches do something."

"No. You just think that."

"What? You saw what happened to Cathal!"

"And he's not one of them!"

"The creatures outside…"

"Moved away from the light, yeah. So you said. But maybe that was because they didn't want to be seen. You think of that? They were hiding. They don't know about lenses and filters. So they see light, and they hide."

"But only on the sol setting."

"Doesn't mean sunlight kills them. They're not some storybook monster, you bloody idiot. They're real."

"So, what, we sit in here and twiddle our thumbs while the air becomes toxic and we run out of food. We wait for a rescue that's never going to come? Don't know about you, Tris, but I don't intend to die in this concrete tomb. I'm not going to hide away like some pathetic child. If I'm going to die, I'd prefer to be doing something useful. Anything more useful than being a bloody whingeing brat of a data-monkey!"

"Enough!" Ryann stepped between the two boys, and noticed that Keelin had done the same. She held out her hands, palm out, one towards Brice, the other facing Tris.

"Enough. Brice, cut the insults. They're childish," she added, using his own insult against him. "And Tris, I said to listen. You have anything to say, you do so in a civilised manner. We work through our problems."

She could hear Tris' breathing clearly, and could taste his adrenaline where it reacted with his lattice. He stood sideways-on, in a fighting stance, and his fists were clenched. But he dropped his arms.

And Brice took his hands from his hips. Interesting, Ryann thought, that he hadn't been in combat pose. With the despair that had been streaming off of him earlier, she didn't know if that was a good sign or not.

"We all know the chances of Haven sending out a rescue crew any time soon are minimal. We need to be proactive about this. And now, we have something to work with—boosters and relay at the pad, relay and another booster on our roof. It's not ideal, and there's a hell of a lot that could go wrong. Tris, you're right—we don't know for certain what sol will do to the creatures. But I saw what happened on the roof, and it seems to keep them back. It's better than nothing."

Ryann paused, conscious of the way three sets of eyes watched her. That unnerved her, but she reminded herself of her position—not a leader, but one of the crew. This was collective work. All she had to do was guide it.

"Going outside will be dangerous. Keelin, you said it was a quarter-k to the pad, right? So ten minutes, maybe fifteen in the conditions out there. Tris, you able to set stuff up here before on-site installation?"

He looked to the neatly stacked equipment on the floor. "Should be able to rig it totally from here, even set a timer to turn on. Just need someone to put it in the right place. And strap a lantern to it. Could train a monkey for that."

"A monkey wouldn't have the guts to go out there with only a couple of torches as defence, " she said quickly, before Brice riled against the comment. "Tris, set up the systems."

"Systems?"

"One for the pad, one for the roof."

Nobody moved.

"We seriously going to do this?"

Ryann suddenly realised that she hadn't even considered *not* doing it. And the energy from that decision excited her.

"I don't want to see Cathal getting any worse. I don't want us to be stuck here. We do what we have to do." She paused, letting that sink in. "How long to set up, Tris?"

"Couple of minutes."

"Good. Then all we need is the brave monkey."

She expected hesitation, or more arguing. But the response came almost instantly. From both sides of the hold out, from the bunks and the stores, the same words came from two mouths as both Brice and Tris spoke.

"I'll do it."

TWENTY-FOUR

Brice turned to Tris, not sure he'd heard right. "You'd go out there?"

Tris looked him up and down. "My tech. And we need this done right."

"What's that supposed to mean?" Brice knew that was too strong, and he stepped back. Tris clenched his fist, and his jaw jutted forward. But then he relaxed.

"Nothing," he said. "Just…just want to make sure it all works. In case there's a problem."

Problems like Brice's lattice screwing up the systems, most likely. But Tris was trying to stay calm. Brice had to meet him on this.

"You willing to go out there with those creatures? You not scared?" He kept his voice level. He didn't want that to sound like a taunt.

Tris looked around, meeting Keelin's gaze and then staring at Brice. "You?"

When he'd stepped on to the roof, he'd felt only calm inevitability. He'd accepted what might happen, and—if he were totally honest with himself—he'd been looking forward to it. But now, everything had changed.

"Terrified," he said, holding Tris' gaze.

"And you still want to go out there?"

"Not want," he said after a pause, "but need. No offence

—honestly—but it's what I do. Physical stuff, walking and carrying things. I'm faster and stronger than you. Even with my screwy lattice. But you're our tech expert. You get those boxes set up, tell me what button to press, and I'll do the manual stuff. I'm the monkey." He tried to laugh, but the sound caught in his throat, and he swallowed a cough.

Tris shook his head. "This involves tech, I should see it through. In case there are any problems. Besides," and here Tris smiled, but it had no warmth, only sadness, "the way your lattice is playing up, you think I'd trust you to even touch any of these boosters?"

Brice knew Tris was right. The way his luck was going, he'd reach the landing pad, turn those things on, and fry the lot of them.

"So you both go," said Ryann, and she stepped closer, hands outstretched, almost touching both Brice and Tris. "Tris to deal with the tech, and Brice to provide cover and protection. We work as a team, right?"

"And I know how to make you safer," Keelin said, stepping forward with a handful of torches. She grinned, and must have sussed to Ryann, because they shared a glint in their eyes. Brice was reminded of training, when a couple of the others would get an idea for a prank. They always had that mischievous look about them too.

When Keelin explained her idea, Brice thought it ridiculous, but as she strapped a torch to his back he understood how it would work. She strapped another to his chest, and slid the covers down on both of them. Light shone all around, bathing the hold-out in wonderful artificial daylight. Ryann did the same to Tris, and they both held their arms out, turning like ridiculous tacky baubles.

He didn't know which of them laughed first, but the sound was infectious.

"Trained for stealth and subtlety, and we're going out like a couple of beacons," Brice said, shaking his head.

"At least you're not dark anymore," Tris said. "And anything I said about you not being bright—guess I'll have to take it back now."

Brice wanted to come back with some other comment, but nothing came to mind, at least nothing that could top how stupid they looked.

"We need something else," Ryann said, and she pointed to the ceiling. Her face was serious, even though she'd been laughing earlier too. "Those things can jump."

"On it," said Keelin, picking up another torch and the tape. "Brice, turn round."

He did so, and felt her taping the third torch to his back. A couple of times it rapped against the back of his head, but Keelin move it down and to his right, and when she thumbed the controls and stepped back, the ceiling above glowed even brighter than it had done before.

"Hey, if I stand like this on the landing pad, I can guide the rescue Proteus in!"

But that thought didn't make him feel any better, and it did not receive the laughter he expected.

"First things first, Brice," said Ryann. "Contact Haven, then worry about rescue."

Keelin strapped a third torch to Tris' back, and now the man did not look ridiculous so much as wrong. He was a dark centre surrounded by light, and he looked alone, just like Brice felt. Tris had said he wasn't dark now, but Brice was. He was an empty void in a sea of brilliance.

Ryann held up a couple of boxes; a booster and a relay. She handed them to Tris, who took them as if she were bestowing a great and terrible gift.

"Set the system up on the roof first," she said. "Let's make sure this works."

Keelin held out a couple of torches. "One to aim at any of those things who get too inquisitive, the other to protect the system," she said.

"I'll need tape, too."

She reached for the roll. Brice shuffled both torches into one hand then held out his other hand, palm up. Keelin looked at the roll of tape, then slotted it over Brice's fingers and pushed it up his wrist.

"Don't let it fall," she said with a smile. Her hand brushed his, and he wanted to grab it. But she was already too far away.

"Ready?" Ryann stood by the rear door. Her face was blank, and she held herself rigid. He felt himself shake when he nodded. The light by his side wobbled as Tris nodded too.

Ryann opened the door.

TWENTY-FIVE

The laughter already felt out of place to Ryann. The last few minutes seemed dream-like, with Tris and Brice joking and working together. It should have filled her with confidence, but instead it left a crack for the doubts to creep in. Not doubts over the decision to do this—with cold logic, she knew it made sense—but she feared the plan would fail. There were too many unknowns.

When Brice reached the top of the ladder and opened the hatch, rain speckled her face. That, she had to admit, felt good. But she couldn't look up, not without calling up some pretty limiting filters. The light Brice and Tris gave off was too strong.

And that was their only protection. She struggled to believe she was letting them go through with this.

"Storm's worse," Brice said.

"Then we do this quickly," Tris said. "Check it works."

Brice barked a laugh. "Not exactly a dry run, though."

Then Brice was through the hatch, and Tris followed. Ryann watched the yellow light swirl, and more rain came down.

<Keep me informed, Tris.>

There was no response for a moment, and Ryann was tempted to call out again, or climb up. Her hand rested on one of the metal rungs.

<There's loads of them!>

Ryann pushed the terror down, redirecting adrenaline.

<Close?>

<*In the trees. But they're hiding from the light. Brice was right.*>

<*Then get the job done. Brice circling you?*>

<*Yeah. Goddamn rain, though!*>

<*It's only water. There was more of it back in the river.*>

That seemed so long ago now. Was it really only a couple of hours?

She heard clicks and thuds over the storm, and pushed into Tris' lattice. His adrenaline pumped, and his heart was loud and strong, if a touch too fast.

<*System in place. Switching it on.*> Ryann sensed the power running through the relay. <*You got that?*>

<*Perfect,*> she sussed. <*Sending message now.*> She tapped into the emergency channel, pushing her signal as identification. She wanted to scream for help, but calmed herself, and stuck to protocol. <*Harris reporting for Lasko. Distress, level one. Respond on receipt, all parties.*>

She pulled up stats, and the data showed the message being sent, broad, across the whole spectrum. She received a ping, but that was from the relay itself, a machine acknowledgement only.

Of course there was no response from Haven. This relay didn't have the power for that. But it would push her message as soon as that second relay was in place.

<*Coming back down.*>

The rain and the noise of the storm both cut off when Brice sealed the hatch. Light flooded the chamber, and water dripped from their clothes.

Keelin was by Cathal's side when they entered the main room. She looked up, but didn't move. It was interesting how she kept one hand under the blanket, resting on his chest.

But if it helped keep the girl calm, Ryann wouldn't interfere.

"Any problems?" she said to the lads.

"Relay seems to be working fine."

"You strapped a torch to it?"

"Of course," said Brice, lifting his arm, the one that still had the reel of tape round his wrist. "This stuff works well."

"Just hope the light keeps those things away," Tris said, then looked sheepish. Ryann understood—while they were all thinking the same thing, speaking it made the doubts real.

"It will," she said with all the confidence she could muster. "And it will work at the landing pad. You need to get the system ready, Tris?"

He nodded. "Sure." Then he turned to Brice. "I'll put it in two packs. Share the load."

"I'll carry it all if you want."

"No. We do this together."

They turned to the storage units, and Ryann stepped across to Keelin.

<*How is he?*> she sussed privately.

The pilot's expression told Ryann more than her words. <*Not good, I think. His skin feels wrong.*>

<*I'll take a look.*>

Keelin withdrew her hand, and shuffled to one side. Ryann wanted to give the girl a hug, but now was not the time. Instead, she called over to Tris and Brice.

"Can we have a different light for a moment? Just need to check on Cathal."

"No problem."

She heard them moving about, and the light in the hold-out dimmed, taking on a blue hue. It felt cold, but Ryann told herself it was only for a moment.

She pulled back Cathal's blanket. He looked so peaceful, with his eyes shut and his face betraying no signs of inner turmoil.

Yet his skin was changing. His forehead felt rough under her fingers, and icy too. The leathery exoskeleton—and that didn't quite describe the blackness, but it came close—stretched high on his neck, reaching up round his jaw. She pulled back his gums, and his teeth were yellow, not the smooth white they had been before. She pulled his upper lip further back, and his canines rose to sharp points.

She let his lips close, all too aware of Keelin at her shoulder.

<*That's bad, isn't it?*>

There was no reason to lie. <*Yes.*>

<What does it mean?>

<It means he needs help.>

<No.>

Ryann spun round. *<No?>*

Keelin didn't move her eyes from Cathal's face. *<Yes, he needs help. But his teeth, and his skin. That means something else. That means he's turning into one of those things, doesn't it?>*

There was no point lying. *<That would appear to be the case. One of those creatures, or something similar.>*

<And he's in here with us.>

<Yes.>

<But we have torches.>

<We do.> Ryann gave nothing, letting Keelin work through this.

<But inside he's still Cathal.>

<I believe so.> Ryann could feel him, in there somewhere. The taste of his trace still existed, beneath the frantic activity and the harsh barriers his lattice was constructing.

<So what do we do?>

Ryann looked across the room, to where Tris was now sealing two packs and handing one to Brice. Neither smiled. They didn't make eye contact.

<We do what we have to do.>

She dropped the blanket back over Cathal, protecting him from the light that would flood the hold-out in a moment. Protecting him from the very thing that they might be called on to use against him.

But not yet. There was still time. She had to believe that.

"You ready?" she asked the boys.

"Ready as we'll ever be," Tris said, shuffling a shoulder to show her the pack he wore. "Boosters linked and primed, relay coded. Just a short walk."

"You got the map?"

He tapped the side of his head. "A half-k. Ten minutes."

"Eight," Brice said. "Let's go for eight."

"Eight," Tris agreed. "We can do that."

"Okay. Torches on." Ryann reached round to their backs while they thumbed the torches strapped to their chests. The hold-out filled with light, and Ryann called up filters to protect her eyes. "While you're in range, keep us informed."

Tris nodded. "And when we've got this system in place, you'll hear us again."

Once more, she stood at the bottom of the ladder as they climbed, and again the rain cascaded down when Brice opened the hatch.

<*Good luck,*> she sussed, and felt terrible for that, terrible that she was relying on luck when she should be confident in their skills and abilities. She should trust her crew.

She climbed after them, and the light from the relay shone into her eyes. She squinted, pulling up tighter filters, and saw Brice lowering himself over the edge of the hold-out. She followed the path of their light as it slid through the trees, sending shadows running and hiding. And she could feel the creatures, could sense…something like pain, but it was like they viewed it with cold logic rather than the vibrant urgency she'd expect from a warth.

But these things were not warths. They were something new.

<*At the landing pad, turning right,*> Tris sussed.

<*I can still see your light.*> But as it moved away from the hold-out, the trees blurred, and the shadows started to smother it.

<*You sitting on the roof in the rain or something?*>

<*Just watching. Good job fixing the relay down, boys.*>

<*Thanks. How Keelin's doing?*>

Interesting question. Ryann couldn't decide if that could be taken at face value, or if Tris was trying to tell her to get inside.

<*Going down to check now.*>

But she waited until she could see their light no more. Only then, after taking a deep breath and feeling a lump in her throat, did Ryann climb inside and close the hatch. The space was dark, the rungs glowing green through her filters, and the water dripping down the walls seemed alien and alive.

Keelin was by Cathal again. She looked up when Ryann entered, and forced a smile.

"They're on their way."

"I heard."

<*There are creatures all around,*> Tris sussed. There was a touch of echo on his voice, and Ryann knew she was receiving it through the relay. <*Can't see them clearly, because they hide too fast. Don't know if they're some of the ones from the hold-out, though.*>

<*You think they're following you?*>

<*Possibly. But they're staying back. Some are up in the trees, though. I don't like how covered this path is.*>

<*Torches pointing up still working?*>

<*Seem to be, although...crap, that was close!*>

<*Tris?*> Keelin called with a gasp.

<*We're fine. Just had one jump, tree to tree. Fairly low down. Think the light kept it off though. Smelt terrible.*>

<*They do,*> Ryann sussed. She glanced at Keelin, noting the relief on her face.

<*Yeah, but this was a smell of burning.*>

<*From the light?*>

<*Could be.*> There was a pause. <*Be good to fry as many of them as possible.*>

But that hesitation belied his bravado. <*Do the job first.*>

<*Will do. But...was that one smoking? Hell! Yeah, we just caught one with a torch, and it stumbled back. Couldn't get to cover. Kept the torch on it, tightened the beam, and the thing's chest started to steam or something. I think this could work!*>

<*Of course it will. You're doing fine, both of you.*>

<*As long as we have these torches, we're good.*>

But the echo on his voice was stronger now. Ryann boosted the signal through her lattice, pushing to the relay.

<*How far along are you, Tris? Just an estimate.*>

<*Checking map. Third of the way there, so ....*>

<*Tris?*>

<*...maybe longer. Goes up...*>

<*Missed that. How much longer?*>

<*Ryann? You still...*>

<Think we're losing connection.>

<...far too many of them...>

<You okay?>

<...can't hear...>

<Tris?>

<...>

Ryann tried again, and she felt rather than heard his voice, distant and filled with static.

<Tris?> Keelin called, her eyes wide.

"Out of range, that's all," Ryann said. "But the torches are working. They'll be fine."

Keelin nodded, but she didn't look convinced.

"They'll be fine," Ryann repeated, and they slipped into silence.

TWENTY-SIX

The path was a sea of mud, and it pulled at Brice's boots with every step. They'd never make the landing pad in eight minutes. Even ten was optimistic.

The trees crowded the path, far too close for comfort. Those creatures had long limbs and sharp claws.

Another one jumped from tree to tree, its hiss angry as it smoldered in the torch beams. Brice followed it with a torch, the burning-flesh stink tasting far better than their normal rancid odour. But then the creature was gone, into the shadows.

The ground rose, and Brice trod through running water now, brown and thick with mud. Tris stumbled a few times, but that wasn't too surprising. He wasn't cut out for this. Gym training only went so far.

This was Brice's speciality, and he had to help Tris. Even if he had to carry the fool. He'd done that with Cathal, hadn't he? And Tris wouldn't be a dead weight. That would make things easier.

But Tris would never agree to that. He'd keep on stumbling, and Brice would have to make do with supporting him as best he could.

The sky burst bright with lightning, the flash tinged green under the canopy of the trees. Silhouettes bulged with possible creatures, and outstretched limbs looked just like branches. The trees were alive.

Tris slipped again, falling to one knee and swinging his other leg out behind his body. It struck Brice on his shin, and he staggered into Tris' back, pushing him further down. There was a squelch as Tris' hand sunk into the mud.

"Watch it!" Tris said, not turning. He pushed himself up as Brice backed off.

Brice bit his lip. He wouldn't say anything. An apology rose in his mind, but he cut that off. Why the hell should he apologise for Tris slipping?

This would have been so much easier on his own. Brice had watched Tris set the system up on the hold-out roof, and there was nothing to it. And the switch he was so worried about? It was mechanical. Faulty lattice or not, there was no way he could screw that up.

Data-monkey shouldn't have been so conceited to think nobody else could do that little bit of the job. He was inflating his own importance, as usual. Bloody idiot.

"How close are we?" Brice asked.

"Close. Shut up and let me follow the map."

The path twisted and turned, but continued to climb. Brice's boot sunk down in the mud, and it squelched as he pulled it free, sounding like a gasp, or a hiss. And maybe it was the sound from the things in the trees.

Then the path widened, and Brice smiled at that. The trees were a good few paces away now. Far enough that one of those things would have to jump into the light to reach him.

One tried, but both Brice and Tris swung their torches at the same time, Tris screaming some kind of childish war-cry. The creature staggered, its body steaming, and fell back into the trees. Tris took a step closer, and Brice was about to say something when the creature stood and ran, further into the forest.

"And don't bother coming back!" Tris yelled. He smiled, and puffed his chest out as he nodded to Brice. "They're not so tough after all," he said as they set off once more.

Brice didn't share Tris' confidence. The torches worked, but what if they broke? Or what if so many of the creatures burst out of the trees?

Then they arrived at the ramp, and Tris uttered a triumphant "Yes!"

The ramp was wide enough for four to walk abreast, and led up to the landing pad, a couple of metres above the surrounding ground. The edges of the pad were steep, so only the ramp gave access. It was smooth, and the rain had coated it in a layer of mud.

Brice leaned into it, pushing with his legs, and his boots slid. He reached forward, grabbing clumps of grass with his hand and pulling hard. By his side, Tris struggled, grunting each time he dug a foot into the mud and pulled with whatever he could find. But Brice was stronger, and he overtook, settling into a rhythm, letting the torches around his wrists fly freely. He breathed with his steps, or stepped with his breaths, and he quickened his pace, refusing to give his feet time to slide.

He reached the top first—of course—and scanned, torches an arm's length from his body. The landing pad itself was large enough to take a couple of craft, and was flat and muddy. The trees started some distance back, but their upper branches reached across the pad, pushed in by the storm. Overhead, Brice could no longer distinguish clouds from the night sky.

Tris staggered up to the top. Brice considered holding a hand out to help, but Tris was bound to take that the wrong way.

"This it?" he asked, and Tris glared at him.

"Course it is. Come on." He stormed off, to the centre of the pad. Brice trailed behind, keeping an eye and both torches on the surrounding forest.

Tris slid his pack off, opened it and removed the equipment. "I need your pack as well."

Brice shuffled it off his shoulders and let it fall to the ground. He continued watching the trees, walking in a tight circle. Tris muttered something, and Brice heard canvas, then clicks as data-boy slotted boosters and relays into place. After a few more rotations, Brice glanced down and saw a red glow.

"Just checking. Give it a chance."

There was movement by the ramp. Brice swung both torches round. A clawed hand slithered in the mud, retreating into the shadows. Brice lowered his beams, and waited, watching. When shadows moved again, he waited still, then darted the torches up.

This time he caught the creature full in its face, and its angry hiss cut through the roar of the storm. Brice held his arms straight as the thing backed away, shielding its eyes.

But it only backed away a step or two. Then it stumbled forward. The hiss turned into a shriek, and in the torchlight Brice saw its flesh start to bubble.

There was a second creature, shielded by the first. It pushed, keeping low, keeping out of sight. But when the first creature fell, steam rising from its bubbling hide, the second cried out and slid back down the ramp.

"We need to move," Brice said.

He sniffed the stench of burning decay, and took a step toward the ramp. There was no more movement. Everything felt … unreal.

"Fine. Made contact. Ryann's talking to Haven." Tris tapped Brice on the shoulder, almost earning himself a punch. "You going to do your stuff with the lantern?"

Brice nodded, and they swapped positions Tris walked round as Brice grabbed the last two torches from the packs. He pulled down the sleeves, then tore off strips of tape and secured them in place. Finally, he thumbed the controls, and shielded his eyes from the brilliance.

"Done," he said, standing. "How are we looking?"

"Fine."

No mention of creatures on the ramp. Maybe Brice had scared them off.

There was another flash of lightning, and the thunder crashed through the forest. Brice flinched—they were exposed up here, and that sounded close.

"You hear that?" Tris said.

"Yeah, thunder." Brice peered towards the ramp. "Lots about, in case you hadn't noticed."

"No, not that. There was a crack."

"Didn't hear anything." Brice listened. Nothing but the storm. "Let's go."

They left the empty packs on the ground, and Brice followed Tris. Bringing up the rear. Watching both their backs.

The ramp was more treacherous on the way down, and Brice turned his feet to the side, angling his body towards the slope. He felt his calves pulling, and he trailed one hand in the mud to keep himself balanced.

Tris didn't have any technique. He tried walking straight down, and after only a couple of steps his arms, already outstretched, started to cartwheel. His body rocked back and forth for a moment, and then he fell.

Brice tried not to laugh.

Tris grunted as he landed on his back, and then he slid down the ramp. Brice followed, pushing into controlled slides, knees bent to absorb as much of the shock as possible.

When they were down, Brice couldn't hold back the laughter any more. Tris was covered in mud. It streaked his face and plastered his hair. He looked like he'd been bathing in the stuff.

"Not funny!" Tris said, and that just made Brice want to chuckle even more.

"You might want to clean your torches," he said, pointing to the one on Tris' chest. Mud covered the lens in a thick, oozing mess, and the light that managed to work through had a dim brown quality, a far cry from the previous yellow-hued warmth.

A sound in the trees made Brice look up sharply. He caught something shifting round a trunk, hiding in the shadows.

"Clean the torches. Come on, Tris! You want those things to come for you?"

That got the message across. Tris looked up, startled, then rubbed at one torch then the other, flicking mud off and smearing the rest. But the sol light burnt through stronger now.

"You do the others." Tris said, turning. Brice wiped the two on his back, the mud warm and slimy, while Tris saw to the torch on his chest.

"Done," he said, when the glow around Tris looked more like daylight. "Let's head back."

Tris nodded, turned, and set off down the path. It twisted and narrowed. Brice thought he remembered it, but he couldn't be sure. The trees seemed closer, and he heard the creatures in the shadows —the rustling of leaves, the creaking of branches, and the low, penetrating sibilance of escaping breath.

Still the rain poured down. The path was a quagmire, and Brice stumbled far too often. He trod on plants and roots whenever he could, but most of the time he trudged through mud, and the pressure was burning his legs.

And then Tris stopped. He pointed along the path, cursing loudly.

At first Brice saw nothing amiss, just more trees. And then he realised what he was looking at. It was a tree, but it wasn't standing.

It lay across the path, blocking the way totally. The thick trunk itself rose over their heads, but that wasn't the worst of their problems. Over the trunk were a tangle of branches and a thick web of leaves. Peering into the greenery, Brice saw shapes shifting, jockeying for position.

"We're screwed," Brice said, and Tris didn't contradict him.

Twenty-Seven

"We're going to get out of this, aren't we?" Keelin looked up with pleading eyes, and Ryann knew what she wanted to hear. But she wasn't going to lie.

"I hope so," she said. "If…when Tris and Brice get the relay in place, we'll be able to contact Haven. Even if we have to sit it out here for a couple more hours, we should be fine."

"You think they'll be okay?"

"They're big boys. They can cope with the forest."

"But can they cope with each other?"

That was a perceptive question, and Ryann gave no answer.

"I could have gone with Tris," Keelin said. "Then you could have kept an eye on Brice. Made sure he was okay, what with being dark."

"Possibly, but as I said, Brice is…trained for more physical stuff. You know that. And if they have something to do, they won't be…diverted into acting like a couple of kids."

That brought a smile to Keelin's face. It was the right thing to say. Better, at least, than what had been in Ryann's mind—that Keelin would not have coped out there. She was barely holding it together as it was.

"Kids is right. Don't know why they act like that."

"You don't?" Maybe this was the distraction Keelin needed.

Keelin shrugged. "Jockeying for position. Some kind of macho crap. Although that's a bit of a throwback, isn't it? Thought we were supposed to have evolved past that."

"Evolution is survival of the fittest. There will always be competition. Everyone wants to be top dog."

"Not me."

"You want to be the best pilot, don't you?"

"Suppose. But that's different. I don't put others down like they do. I don't start fighting just to prove a point."

"No? How often do you take breaks when you're tired?"

"I take breaks!"

"But only when…only when someone reminds you to. Admit it—you're a good pilot, and you want others to know it."

Keelin looked away and shrugged. That was answer enough.

"But it's natural," Ryann continued, knowing she needed to keep this positive. "Don't let it bother you. Just watch out that it doesn't cause problems."

"What about you? Can't see you being that petty, Ryann. You're always looking out for us, like a … like we're important to you."

Ryann filled in the word Keelin had avoided, and it hurt. Did the girl see Ryann as a mother-figure? Did that make Cathal a father-figure? Yes, that made sense, but Ryann wasn't old enough…she wasn't ready…she wasn't a mother. She held a more senior position, but she was still just another crew member.

But she pushed her annoyance to one side. "That's because you are important to me. This crew's family. And I want it to be the best in Haven."

"We are."

"Of course."

Only we're not in Haven, Ryann thought. We're trapped in the forest, and our commander is turning into some kind of monster. Two of us are walking through the trees, protected by a few torches against creatures that can kill warths, and two of us are talking girl-talk because we're not able to do anything else. And in a few hours time, we could all be dead. Or worse.

"You sense Tris or Brice at all?" Keelin asked.

Ryann shook her head. She'd kept her connection to the relay open, but so far hadn't got a single ping.

"How long before they get that relay set up?"

"Should be there about now."

As if on cue, a voice reached into her head.

<Ryann, you hearing me?>

Keelin grinned, and Ryann felt the relief wash over her. Or maybe that was Ryann's own relief.

<I hear you, Tris. Take it the relay's in place?>

<All set. Looks like a bloody beacon with the torches, too. Probably easy to see when the Proteus comes for us.>

<Probably. But don't jump the gun. This thing reach Haven?>

<Pretty sure. Give it a go.>

Ryann sent a protocol message. *<Haven, this is Ryann Harris, second to Cathal Lasko. Are you receiving?>*

There was nothing for a moment, then a voice flowed into her mind. *<Receiving. Expected you back hours ago, Harris.>*

Ryann shook. She exhaled, unaware until now that she'd been holding her breath. She wanted to cry. She wanted to hug Keelin.

But she took a breath and calmed the adrenaline racing through her system. *<Had a few problems. We could do with a hand.>*

<Okay. You got a report ready?>

<Sending it now.>

Of course she had a report ready. All the thoughts, all the data—everything had been building in Ryann's storage, and she'd returned to it almost as a comfort, pulling phrases out to create a summary. Until this point, she hadn't even realised she was compiling a report. It was simply something she did.

<You got it?> she sussed as she pushed it through. Ryann wanted to use the man's name, but that was not protocol. She was contacting Haven, not Quin Barberis. He could use her name—second name only, though—but for this communication, he was simply 'Haven'.

<Got it. Scanning. Lasko's injured? Sorry, can't make out how serious this is. You say he's stable?>

<*Stable, yes. But serious. He needs more than I can give him.*>

<*Understood. I've logged your position. Take it you want us to go for you, not your Proteus?*>

<*Correct.*> Ryann wouldn't allow herself to become frustrated by these questions. They were protocol. They ensured clear communication.

<*And there's something else out there? Haven't...that's not linking to anything on our systems. You sure about this?*>

<*Definitely.*> She felt the need to elaborate. <*New creature, extremely dangerous.*>

<*And, what, they're repelled by light?*>

<*Just sol setting. At least, as far as we can figure out. That's why any rescue craft need to come in with their arcs burning with sol. For their own protection as much as ours.*>

<*Understood.*> But Ryann picked up on the pause, and knew Quin would be wondering about the validity of the data, or even of her own sanity. <*Passing this on.*> Again, that was protocol. The report, and request for assistance, were now in the system, and there would be others deciding what course of action to take.

<*Just sit tight, Ryann. We'll get you back home.*>

The slip from protocol shocked her, and she didn't know if it was good or bad.

<*Thanks,*> she sussed. And realised she was still shaking.

Twenty-Eight

Brice stared up at the tree. "We go over it?" he asked, even though he knew that wasn't an option. Even if they could cut through with their knives, the creatures waited inside.

"What do you think?" Tris snapped back.

"There another way round?"

"I'm checking. Stop asking stupid questions."

Brice held his hands up in surrender and stepped back a pace, then played his torches over the trees. Shadows shifted all around, and up high branches moved through more than the wind. All it would take was a handful of the creatures to drop, and Brice and Tris would be done for. Even if the first ones burnt up, the ones behind would have some shelter from the light. Enough to take a few swipes with their claws. And that was all it would take.

They should have walked faster. If Tris had picked up the pace and trusted his feet, they could have cleared this path before the tree fell. If he hadn't wanted to check everything so many times, they'd probably be back at the hold-out by now, out of the storm, with help on its way. But no, he had to make sure. He had to go slow and careful. And now, his hesitation had screwed them.

"There's another track," Tris said. "Come on." He pushed past Brice, heading back towards the landing pad. Brice shrugged and followed.

After a couple of paces, Tris turned to the right. There was a path of sorts, but Brice thought of claws sweeping out, and he shuddered.

"You sure?" He asked.

"No other way. What, you scared?"

Brice shook his head, even though he was. But so was Tris. Brice could practically smell the fear pouring off him.

"Come on then." Tris turned, swallowing, and made his way into the trees. Brice followed once more.

Branches closed in all around. That stopped the worst of the rain, but now each drop of water was bigger, and as each one struck him Brice thought of what else was up there. A roar filled his ears, and he could no longer tell what was the forest, what was the creatures, and what was the blood rushing around his body. His muscles tightened with the too-warm after-glow of adrenaline. His fingers gripped the torches, and he moved in a crouch, ready to run.

As if he could outrun those things.

"You know where you're going?" he asked.

"Shut up."

The track dissolved into little more than a twisting gap between angry branches. They clawed at his face, and pulled at his arms. Creepers lay in wait, tight against his boots, and Brice staggered with every step. His legs burnt from the effort of pushing through the undergrowth.

And he expected every step to be his last.

Brice wondered if he'd feel the claws slice into him, or if realisation would only come once his blood had run free. He tensed, knowing he'd never be ready for the fangs sinking into his skin, ripping through his flesh.

"Trees open up here," Tris said, his voice full of relief.

Brice looked through Tris' circle of light, and his chest thudded with relief. A few steps more, and the track became a path once more. The trees parted, and they stepped into a small clearing. Now, if the creatures wanted to reach Brice, they would have to step into the torch-light.

He realised that it was not actually a clearing, but an intersection. The path they took dipped down, then rose ahead, continuing through the trees. Crossing this was a wider path, running along a depression. Only this wasn't a path any more.

Tris stopped.

"That was our path," he said quietly, his voice cracking. His arm shook as he pointed to the dip.

Their route lay along a trench, or maybe it was a big ditch. But the rain had been falling for too long, filling the ditch with mud. But not the mud that clung to other paths. Not mud that they could walk through.

This mud was moving. The path was a brown, oozing river.

"Any other way?" Brice asked.

"Checking."

The stench of the mud was almost overpowering, the taste hitting the back of Brice's throat and making him gag.

"If we can get over, that track can take us back."

"Rope?"

"You got any?"

Brice shook his head as the brown river slid past. It was almost hypnotic, the way the gunk folded over itself. Not liquid, but not solid either. He imagined stepping into the river and sinking into the ooze, leisurely feeling the mud encase his body. He wondered if it would be warm.

He wondered how far down he'd go.

And Brice realised he couldn't see the ground beneath the mud. He had no idea of the depth.

Brice turned to the trees, searching for something to use. He reached out and pulled, and a branch tore free with a satisfying crack. It was smooth and old, more of a pole than a branch.

"You going to make us a bridge?" Tris' tone was mocking. Brice chose to ignore him. Stupid comments wouldn't get them any further.

He crept down the bank, to the edge of the mud. With one hand grasping some kind of fern, and a part of him terrified that it would break, Brice reached out and pushed the branch into the slow river. He felt the mud sucking angrily at it, but he held his wrist firm and pushed the pole down. And down.

Even before his hand reached the mud itself he knew this was pointless. He released the branch, and it slid beneath the surface and disappeared.

"You finished playing?"

Brice took a deep breath, closing his eyes. "Checking the depth," he explained. "Just in case … but it's too deep."

"Could've told you that before."

"At least I'm trying." Brice straightened up and stepped away from the bank.

"Fat lot of good it's doing us." Tris took a step closer, the torch on his chest shining into Brice's eyes. "That's all you ever do, isn't it? You try. About time you started doing instead."

Brice blinked. That made so little sense. But before he could respond, data-monkey was talking again.

"You fired at that warth because you were trying to help, and they attacked. You tried to turn the bloody hold-out lights on, and totally screwed the power. Every time you try, things get worse." He jabbed a finger at Brice, the torch swinging from his wrist. Brice felt it slam against his chest. "You're a liability. It's a wonder any of us are still alive with you around."

Brice's eyes watered from the light, but he stared at Tris, refusing to blink. Tris' beady little eyes flickered, too close together, and Brice hated them. He hated Tris, with his cloying, sickly breath and his stupid padded muscles, and his superior attitude. He hated everything the techie stood for, everything that was wrong with the company and this job and this mission. He hated how Keelin looked up to Tris, and how everyone looked down on Brice himself. He hated this bloody forest and this storm and the way those creatures were playing with them. He hated being out here, and most of all he hated Tris.

The punch was sharp, and the impact shuddered through Brice's arm. Tris staggered back, one hand rising to his throat as he struggled for breath. His eyes grew wide and fearful.

Brice didn't move. His knuckles stung, and the muscles in his arm were too tight, but that all felt oh so good.

Tris gurgled, trying to speak. He coughed, doubling over, and Brice heard him pull in a ragged breath. And then he charged.

But Brice was ready. But all he had to do was side-step, and Tris' swinging fist missed its target. The torch, following through, caught Brice squarely on the shoulder, but when he grunted it was more from shock than from pain.

And Tris was off-balance. It was easy for Brice to sweep a leg out. Tris landed with a squelch and rolled into some of the ferns.

Seeing him on the ground freed Brice's tongue. "I'm trying to get us out of here," he said. He took a breath and stepped back. "I'm trying. That's all I can do."

Tris grabbed a handful of foliage, and he breathed deeply. Mud coated his jacket, and water poured over his face. He didn't look at Brice. Then he pulled his legs in, preparing to stand.

All Brice had to do was push, and Tris would be back in the mud. But his anger had already gone.

"I'm trying my best," he said again, and offered his hand. It shook, and Brice wanted to believe that was the muscles in his arm, still recovering from the punch. "We need to work together."

Tris looked at Brice's hand as if he'd never seen it before. Then he nodded, and reached up with his own hand. It was warm, and mud oozed between their fingers, but Brice curled his grip round and pulled back, letting his weight help Tris to his feet.

Neither of them spoke. Brice could think of nothing to say. He felt the rain running down his skin, leaving trickles of coolness behind. Tris must be feeling the same. The techie's hair hung low over his forehead, plastered to his skin. His mouth opened and closed a couple of times. Brice saw that his neck was red. When Tris gulped, he winced in pain.

And then Tris' head jerked to one side, and he cursed loudly. He brought a hand up to his temple, and Brice saw blood. Not much, but the rain-water pulled it free.

A shape moved to his right, and Brice instinctively ducked. But the swinging branch grazed his head, pulling his neck back.

Another branch swung, but he was ready now, and he stepped

to one side, sweeping an arm round to deflect the blow. His torch-light swam into the trees, and there was a hiss as a shadow backed away.

"They're attacking us with branches?" A fern slapped towards him, and he let it hit, moisture coating his face. But then another branch slammed into his leg, and he stumbled.

Tris turned, jerking as his body took blows from the branches. But he was laughing.

"This all you got?" He yelled, swatting a branch away with his arm. Brice moved closer to him, ducking as another branch swung his way, and as a fern frond slapped against Tris' head. He laughed. "Bloody leaves?"

That was when the rock slammed into Tris' head.

He spun, and an arc of blood flew from his temple. He staggered, colliding with Brice and pushing them both back. Brice brought a foot round, but it slipped away, and he felt his thigh wrench as he toppled.

They fell. Tris landed on Brice, pushing the air from his lungs, and Brice's head flew back into soft mud. Something stuck his leg, then an arm. He knew it wasn't branches now. Each hit was like a punch, small and sharp, the pain short-lived but intense.

Brice pushed Tris away, and turned face-down as the pummelling continued. He jerked when the blows caught his spine, and brought his hands up to protect his head. Maybe he yelled out.

Something crashed, sharp and clear, and the light over his shoulder dimmed. He felt the skin on his hand dance, and pin-pricks of pain flared up.

Tris cried out, with no words Brice could make out. The man rose, arms over his head. Then he staggered, spasming as more rocks hit. His arms flailed, and he went down once more. Brice saw his body slip, gravity pulling it down the slope.

Brice pushed himself to his feet, ignoring the rocks that struck him. He launched himself forward, throwing a hand out, even as Tris slid further down the bank. He called out, and Tris looked up, his eyes glowing bright against his mud-smeared face.

The next rock slammed into Brice's head, and he toppled forward. Tris' terrified eyes filling his fractured vision. The light burnt Brice's eyes, so bright it was black. Nausea rose as he fell.

But he didn't stop moving. The ground slid away, and he couldn't stop himself following it.

He only just thought to close his mouth before the mud engulfed him.

Twenty-Nine

"You think they believe us?" Keelin asked. "I mean, about those creatures. And Cathal."

"They have the data now." Ryann knew she was avoiding the question.

"And you told them about the light. That's good. And they know where we are. And that we need urgent help."

Ryann nodded, letting Keelin babble. Her voice ricocheted between excitement and terror.

"Someone in Haven must know about those creatures. They've probably already got an antidote. They're probably preparing a medi-bay right now. Don't you think, Ryann? They're going to make it all better. They have to." Then, quieter, she repeated herself. But it was more of a question now. "They have to."

Then she looked up, her eyes bright. "When do you think the boys will be back?" she asked.

"You could ask them."

That brought a smile to Keelin's face, although Ryann wasn't sure it was genuine. It might have been a mask. And it frustrated Ryann that she was so unsure about this. She thought her understanding of the pilot was better than this.

<*Hey, Tris, Brice. You there?*> Keelin almost sounded breezy.

<*On our way back now. Be good to get out of this rain.*>

Keelin jerked at Tris' voice, but Ryann knew her smile was genuine now.

<Brice okay too?>

<He's fine.>

<You hear me, Brice? Give Tris a nod if you can. Tris, he nodding?>

<Don't know. I'm trying to figure out our path. We've had to take a detour.>

And only now did Ryann hear the hesitation, and the panic simmering beneath Tris' words.

<Problems?> she sussed, dreading the response.

<Path blocked. I've got another route, though. Be back before you know it. You got through to Haven?>

That sounded like he was sure of himself, but Ryann knew that was a mask. But she followed where he led the conversation. *<We got through. We're in the system.>*

<In the system,> Tris sussed dismissively. *<Suppose that's good. See you in a bit.>* And Tris cut communication.

Keelin looked worried. "You think Brice is okay?"

"He'll be fine."

Ryann cringed inside as she said those words. And it hurt even more when Keelin nodded in agreement. It was what Keelin wanted to hear, but that didn't excuse the…not lie, but the way Ryann skirted round what she really thought.

And what was that? Logically, she knew that Tris was still walking, and he'd said he knew a way back. Ryann had no reason to believe Brice was not with him. They were surrounded by light. They *should* be fine.

Yet Ryann was filled with dread. A part of her never expected to see them again. Hell, a part of her never expected to see Haven again.

But she couldn't admit that to Keelin. The girl would fall apart.

<Ryann, you there?>

The voice startled Ryann, and at first she thought it was Tris again. But this voice was female. It was deep, and sure of itself. Of course she recognised it.

<I'm here, Arela. Didn't expect you to call.> Ryann knew that wasn't formal enough, and that this wasn't the correct protocol for a

communication from Haven's chief, but at the moment she didn't care. Besides, she'd always thought of Arela as a kind of friend, once you got through the layers of bureaucracy.

But there were protocols and systems, and Arela had to follow them closer than most. Calling Ryann up like this was…not how things were done.

<Always look out for my people. You know that. Especially ones with a problem.>

<A problem. That's putting it lightly.> Ryann felt the signal Arela was using. It was tight, and she knew the chief was alone. Maybe she wasn't even in her office, but was calling from her quarters.

<So I understand. Read your report—well, scanned most of it. We've got medics preparing for Cathal, and we're moving as fast as we can.> She paused. <But these creatures…I'm intrigued.>

That was an odd choice of words, and Ryann felt her skin chill as blood rushed to her brain. But before she could dwell on it, Arela was talking again.

<Tell me, Ryann, what do they feel like when you sense them?>

That was incredibly blunt. Arela kept her tone light, but a question like that spoke of seriousness. Ryann took a moment of contemplation before responding. *<I'm not sure I can put it in words. They move, and they have a hint of life, but at the same time they feel empty.>*

<Like tech?>

<I can't feel tech,> she sussed, choosing her words with care. Arela was fishing for something.

<But you reach out to others' lattices. That's tech, surely.>

Ryann could have explained how tech was a conduit for sensations. A lattice was a delivery system, not a thing in itself. And it worked so intimately with the body that it was near impossible to tell where the biological ended and the artificial began.

She could have explained all of this, but Arela had trained as a tracker. She understood this already.

<What are you getting at, Arela? What can you tell me?>

<*Just gathering data. There's only so much in a report.*>

That might have been a dig. Of course reports only gave the hard facts. Ryann was very careful with her words. But Arela could read between the lines.

And Ryann could do the same. <*What can you tell me, Arela?*>

Arela didn't respond straight away, and for a moment Ryann feared she had been too blunt. Her nerves were rising. She needed to stay calm. She needed to be friendly, not confrontational.

But Arela was still there. <*Officially, we know nothing of those creatures, Ryann,*> she eventually sussed, and her voice was measured and strong. <*There are no records in Haven's data-banks.*>

Ryann heard what Arela wasn't saying all too clearly. <*But unofficially?*>

Arela paused again, then sussed, <*You understand this conversation isn't happening. These words never passed between us. Clear?*>

<*Clear.*>

<*I hear any indications to the contrary, I will deny them most strongly. And you know that evidence will not be forthcoming.*>

Ryann understood perfectly, although the threat hurt on a personal level. Arela had total access to Haven's data banks, including what every individual stored through their lattice. If Ryann had been recording this conversation, Arela could wipe the recording and amend any affected records.

But she must know that Ryann would not put her in such a position. Her distrust could not be aimed at Ryann, but at anyone else who might be listening in, if that were even possible.

It wasn't like Arela to be paranoid. Not without good reason.

<*I understand,*> she said.

<*I know.*> Arela's tone softened a fraction, and Ryann could picture her smiling. <*And I do trust you, Ryann. I wouldn't be this frank if I didn't.*> That sounded almost like an apology.

There was a pause—Ryann could think of no response—and then Arela continued. <*I'm in an interesting position, Ryann. I have access to deeper records than most, but I also hear things. Things that the data cannot back up. I hear rumours, and half-truths, and downright lies. Sometimes, it's hard to tell these apart. And sometimes, I would prefer it if the truths were the lies.*>

<*I understand.*> And Ryann also saw how Arela was building to something.

<*Kaiahive's a gargantuan company. You know this. The Haven project's a fraction of a fraction of their concerns. Nobody can know of all the projects they run.*>

<*Yes.*> Ryann could see where this was going. <*And I'm sure many of those projects are ones they would like to keep from prying eyes.*>

<*Exactly.*> Her voice changed, becoming softer, like silk. Ryann recognised it as the voice of a manipulator, and listened for the scalpel beneath the silk. <*Tell me, when you feel those creatures, are they more human or more animal?*>

Ryann answered slowly, drawing the truth from deep inside, pushing emotions away. <*They do not have the life-flow of either human or animal, but their traces have similarities to both.*>

<*Don't be so evasive. I'm trying to help. What part feels human?*>

<*I'm not sure what you want me to say, Arela. They show a superior intelligence. Is that what you're getting at?*>

Ryann heard the chief sigh, and when she next spoke the words were clear and slow. <*Do you feel evidence of anything like a lattice when you sense the creatures?*>

Yes. But Ryann couldn't admit that. She couldn't accept what that meant. So she remained silent.

<*Of course you do,*> Arela continued. <*You're one of the best trackers I've ever known, Ryann.*>

Ryann split her focus, and reached out, as much as she could, beyond the walls of the hold out. She used the relay, and she searched for the creatures. Of course, they surrounded her like a fog, but she pulled in her range, focusing tighter, narrowing down on an individual. And there, incredibly faintly, she felt movement, like a pulse. Yet it was slow and sluggish, and that was not the driving force here. No, there was something else, a subcutaneous flow through the whole body.

Yes, she could feel evidence of a lattice. Decayed and twisted, but still a lattice.

<*Those things are human?*> She looked to the blanket covering Cathal, and shuddered.

<*Were. I don't know the exact classification now.*>

<*But...how?*>

<*I know none of this, Ryann. There is no way I can back up my suspicions. If I tried, there are those who would silence me.*> She paused, and Ryann imagined black-clothed operatives, or political manoeuvring. <*But I need to keep my people safe. I would be failing in my job if I did not equip them with the knowledge I felt they required.*>

<*So what do I need to hear?*>

<*To be honest, I'm not sure. But you're smart, Ryann. I'll tell you what I know, but you'll have to figure out how to use it. Okay?*>

<*Okay.*> And, of course, it wouldn't be everything Arela knew. Or even suspected.

When Arela next spoke, her voice flowed easily, and Ryann pictured her leaning back in a chair. <*You know about the body-snatchers, Ryann? Back in the early days of medical science? There were no labs, no virtual simulations. All knowledge came from studying bodies, so body-snatchers were hired to obtain cadavers. Officially, they dug up freshly-buried corpses. But unofficially, many people lost their lives to further our understanding of biology.*>

<*I'm familiar with the stories.*> Ryann could also see where Arela was going with this.

<*Of course you are. And I'm sure you can appreciate the justifications.*>

<*The sacrifice of the few for the benefit of the many. It's standard medical philosophy.*>

<*Yes. But it doesn't only apply to medicine. It's a business concept too—start-up costs might be high, but the rewards will*

repay them many times over. You take an initial hit in order to reap the benefits later.> Arela paused, and when she spoke again her tone became harsh. <*Tell me, Ryann—what is the company's greatest achievement to date?*>

That was obvious, but Ryann was already leaping ahead.

<*The company could only do so much lattice research virtually. Eventually, they had to use people.*> Arela said nothing, waiting for Ryann to continue. <*And not all that research would be successful.*>

<*Trial and error. Bedrock of science. You understand?*>

Ryann's stomach churned. <*So what happened to the...test subjects when the research failed?*>

<*Success and failure are fluid terms. Failure is a part of the learning process. Everything is ongoing.*>

<*Just like lattice development.*> Of course the company were still pushing for improvements. <*But if people died...*>

<*People die all the time.*> Arela paused. <*But death isn't the issue here.*>

<*No.*> Ryann looked at the blanket covering Cathal, like a shroud. <*Maybe death isn't the worst that could happen.*>

That would explain why those creatures—those failed tests—had an echo of a lattice. But it still left too many questions. The elongated limbs, the stretched jaws and the fangs and claws—these were physical changes. The lattice might help a body's natural processes, but it couldn't alter physiology to such an extent. The idea was…it was beyond preposterous. It was the stuff of bad horror stories, or old folk tales.

The stink from Cathal's wound hit the back of her throat, but it no longer made her feel so nauseous. She wanted to believe that was a sign of his infection receding, but she knew the reality. She was becoming used to the stench.

It was possible to become accustomed to death. Ryann's medical training had taught her that. Death was a part of life, a part of a cycle. And sometimes, death was a release. She'd held the hands of patients, both old and young, as they'd slipped away, and she'd felt their passing. Even without the enhancements the company would give her later, she was attuned to others, and she knew that, sometimes, letting go could be a comfort.

But what if it was not possible to let go? What if someone were trapped in the endless agony of their condition?

She thought of the black emotions that rolled off those creatures, and she wondered how much of that was from the pain they felt inside.

<*So what can we do?*> Ryann sussed. <*Does any of this help us?*>

<*Understanding can always help. You've told me that enough times, Ryann. Learn, understand, then act.*>

<*But right now?*>

<*I don't know. Your hold-out's secure. And the whole thing with the sol light—I'd never heard any rumours about that. You're already outsmarting them. I know this is going to sound cruel, but if I had to choose anyone to put in this situation, I'd choose you. If anyone can figure out those things, it's my old friend Ryann Harris.*> Her tone shifted, becoming stronger, but also distant. This was Arela the chief. <*Sit tight. We're coming for you.*>

<*Thanks.*>

<*Anything for a friend. We'll chat when you're back.*>

Ryann felt the slight hesitation in that last sentence, and the urgency behind it. Yes, they would talk, but it couldn't be a friendly chat. They would talk of creatures and lattices, and of the horrors Kaiahive had unleashed.

THIRTY

The mud wrapped around Brice, like slow hands dragging him down. He shut his eyes, and clamped his lips tight, but the cloying smell still hit the back of his throat. He felt the ooze under his jacket, against his flesh.

He pushed his hands out, and when one broke the surface he forced his body round, pushing with his legs. The mud provided enough resistance, and when he felt rain pummelling the top of his head, he tilted his neck back and opened his mouth, gulping in air.

Brice coughed as he swallowed mud, and his stomach convulsed. He pushed with his arms and legs, forcing his head higher. The mud pulled him down, but he fought it. He kicked and grabbed, and then he found a branch, or a root. Something that remained firm in his hand, anyway.

Slowly he dragged himself from the mud. Slime crawled from his ears, and the mud sucked at the hole his body had left.

He found a tree trunk and turned himself around, bringing his knees up to his chest. His body convulsed. The mud slithering down his body was warm, but it left a coldness in its wake.

His back pressed firmly against the tree, and that told him something important. The two torches were no longer there. The torch on his chest hung to one side, the tape flapping uselessly, and it wouldn't stick when he tried to push it back in place. And only then did he realise that the glass was broken, and that it gave off no light. He thumbed the controls uselessly.

One torch still hung from his right wrist. He could feel its weight, but he could see no light. He didn't try the controls, because he didn't want to know if it was broken.

His left wrist was bare.

Brice sat in the dark, his chest rising and falling. He pulled air into his lungs until he felt light-headed. He concentrated on his body, and the numbness slowly gave way to patches of throbbing pain. His shoulder felt twice the size it should have been, and it resisted when he tried to roll it forward. His head burnt with a sharp pain, over an eye but spreading wide.

The rest of his body wasn't much better, but he knew he couldn't stay like this. He had to move.

Brice sat in the dark, listening to the sounds of the forest.

Rain fell and wind blew. The storm continued. The mud gurgled past his feet, and branches shuddered all around.

Brice stood, using the tree for support. His eyes must have become accustomed to the dark now, because he could make out the undulating ground that was the river of mud. Everything else was trees and branches and leaves.

Brice grabbed a branch and pulled himself round, away from the mud. Then he moved to the next tree, then the one just past that. Slowly, carefully, Brice worked his way through the forest. As far as he could tell, back the way he'd come. Back to where he'd fallen into the mud.

Where they'd both fallen.

Brice forced himself onward. Rain fell and wind blew. He could hear the mud gurgling, just to his left. Branches rubbed and shuddered all around. And something cried out.

Brice stopped, unsure if he'd heard that last sound. Or what it was. Then it came again, a yell, sharp and angry. It came from ahead. Brice stared, and thought he saw a light flickering.

He didn't run, because his legs wouldn't move that fast, but he grabbed branch after branch and thrust his boots through the undergrowth. Tris shouted again, and the light jerked about in the shadows.

"Hold on!" Brice yelled, but the words fell at his feet with a cough, and he stumbled. His legs gave way. Sharp thorns ripped into his hand. But he gripped the branch, the pain clearing his mind. He grunted as he kicked forward, keeping his balance. And now he did run.

The light was up ahead, dancing in the trees, and Tris screamed and yelled. Through the shadows, Brice saw shapes moving.

"I'm coming," he managed to shout, and maybe Tris answered. A crash of thunder echoed through the trees, and the flash of lightning illuminated Tris.

And the creatures.

Tris stood in a wide path, his arms outstretched, a torch in each hand. But all around him were the dark, leathery creatures. They leaned in, and through the rain Brice could hear their guttural hisses. Their arms were wide, and their claws flashed in the light from Tris.

But the light was wrong. It was dim, and instead of yellow the glow was green, or maybe brown. And the creatures were not afraid of it.

Brice could smell them now, their rancid stench cutting through the stink of the mud. He felt it pushing into his mouth, and he wanted to vomit, his chest heaving. But he forced himself forward.

One of the creatures lunged towards Tris, and claws slashed down. Tris staggered, his cry sharp and high-pitched, and his right arm dropped. Something red sprayed from his shoulder.

Brice pushed forward, his fist clenched and his arm pumped. He aimed for the back of the closest creature, and his knuckles drove into the thing's head. There was a crack, and he didn't know if that was his bones or not, but the burst of pain drove him on.

He spun, swinging for another creature. He caught this one with his other hand, his torch colliding with its neck. The creature staggered, or maybe that was Brice.

And then a black shape flew through the air, and Brice crashed to one side, his boots sliding from under him. His head jerked back, and he hit the ground.

Everything slowed. But Brice couldn't move.

Tris' cries grew more intense, losing any semblance of words, and the yells were mixed with sobs now. The shadows swarmed round him, consuming the dim light. And then they fell on him.

Brice heard something shatter as the light disappeared. The shadows merged, but the blackness undulated. There was a sharp crack, and an animalistic scream that burst through Brice's head. And then Tris' cry stopped.

There was a rustling, rubbing sound that told Brice the creatures were moving against one another, but he caught another noise beneath this. A slurping, or maybe a sucking. It stopped for a moment, then continued.

The shapes moved. Brice couldn't see them clearly, but they pulled away from Tris. The sucking sound stopped, and then they moved away, fading into the trees. Their hisses dissolved into the rain, and then only their stench remained.

Brice rose to his feet, one hand grabbing a tree for balance. What little vision he had swam violently, and he was forced to close his eyes for a moment. He breathed, through his nose but he could still taste the creatures. And something else. Something coppery and sharp.

The forest and the path were nothing but dark shadows.

Brice gripped his one remaining torch in his hand, and he thought of the pale light coming from Tris. He remembered how the mud had coated his torch's lenses.

Brice cleaned his own torch as best he could. He spat, using the mucus to clean more of the mud off. The glass still felt gritty, and he knew it wasn't perfect, but it was the best he could do.

And then he thumbed the controls.

The light was weak, but the comforting yellow glow was the most beautiful thing he'd ever seen.

Brice shone it around the path. The undergrowth had been flattened, and something glinted in the light. One of Tris' torches, smashed and useless. The other torch lay a little further off, and that too was broken.

But there was no sign of Tris.

Brice played his light through the trees, following the path of trampled foliage. He didn't understand why the creatures would take Tris, but that was what had happened. They had attacked him, then abducted him. And Brice was on his own.

He thumbed the torch controls, extinguishing the light. Darkness surrounded him. He breathed deep, letting his thoughts settle. He needed to concentrate. He needed to look at things objectively. Like Ryann or Cathal would. He needed to recall, then analyse.

The creatures had taken Tris, and he could see the path they had taken. He could follow.

That was an absurd idea. Brice would never get through the creatures. He'd already tried, and he'd failed. The creatures had flung him to one side like they were swatting a fly. They'd focused solely on Tris. Brice was nothing more than an annoyance.

He couldn't go after Tris. But he couldn't stay here either. Brice put his hands on his hips and imagined how Cathal might think, the situation running through his head.

Tris was gone, and Brice was alone. But the others were at the hold-out, and with the relay and boosters they must have contacted Haven.

Help was on its way. All Brice had to do was walk back to the hold-out.

Trees surrounded him. There was no map in his head, and they were far from the path they'd taken earlier. But they had walked uphill to reach the landing pad. That meant the hold-out was lower down. And water—and the mud it carried—always flowed downstream.

Grabbing branches for support, Brice returned to the mud-filled trench and started to walk.

Thirty-one

"They're on their way," Keelin said.

Ryann covered Cathal with the blanket again, and flicked the lantern back to sol. Cathal's condition was deteriorating.

"A Proteus," Keelin continued, moving into Ryann's line of sight. "Should be here in about ten minutes."

"That's fast." Almost impossible, Ryann thought, especially with the storm. Maybe she should have monitored communications rather than leaving that up to Keelin. But the girl needed something to take her out of the hold-out. She needed a focus.

"It's not coming from Haven. You remember Nyle and Osker?"

Ryann did, although she hadn't given them a thought. They were in a hold-out not too far away—ten minutes flying time, apparently—on some reduced-crew training mission. But that meant they were in the forest.

"Any of these creatures near them?" Ryann asked.

"Didn't ask, but I don't think so."

So it was only her crew that were being targeted. She didn't know if that was good or bad.

"They know about sol, though?"

"Haven told them. I reiterated. Think Nyle was a bit annoyed at being told twice. I told him it was important."

Keelin's tone was conversational, with none of the fearful shaking it had held earlier. But she shuffled about as she spoke, and used her hands to emphasise her words—not something she normally did. Ryann pushed gently, reaching for the girl's lattice.

As she expected, Keelin's heart beat fast, and her breathing was fast and shallow. She was still terrified. The relaxed manner was a front—no, a way of coping. Help was on its way, but it would be a long ten minutes. A lot could happen in that time.

"You speak to Osker?"

"Just Nyle. Osker was checking supplies or something." She shrugged. "Guess he was leaving temp-command to Nyle anyway."

Temp-command. Ryann hadn't even considered that term, but it was what she was doing. With Cathal…incapacitated, she was in charge temporarily.

And that meant she should be the one to communicate with Nyle. But protocol would dictate she referred to him as Patera, and he would call her Harris. They would need to be formal, and stifled.

Better to let Keelin talk to him, pilot to pilot. That was her decision, as temp-command.

"Did he say anything about the weather?" Ryann asked, keeping things light.

"Said the storm's getting worse. But he says it's better to fly than to be cooped up in a concrete box."

"They know about our power issues? They know they can't come to the front door?"

"Told them. They didn't seem too surprised. Seems everyone's having glitches. Even Haven's ready to switch to back-up systems."

Ryann glanced at the blanket covering Cathal. Even on back-up, Haven would keep medical facilities running. All she had to do was get her crew back. When Nyle and Osker landed, they'd get Cathal on board, and they'd all get back to the base.

As long as Tris and Brice turned up on time.

She pushed, through the relay on the roof.

<Tris? How's things?> She kept it conversational. *<How long before you're back?>*

There was no reply.

<Tris? Brice? You receiving?>

Keelin's voice joined in, and Ryann cursed herself for keeping communications wide. <*You two need to get back here. Help's on its way.*>

Nothing.

Ryann pushed further, and there was something. It wasn't tangible, but she caught a trace, so faint that it almost didn't exist.

"How come we can't reach them?" Keelin's face was pale. Ryann shook her head and held up a hand. That wouldn't comfort Keelin, but Ryann needed to concentrate.

She followed the phantom trace, and it had the flavour of decay. It reminded her of Cathal's wound, and of…yes…the creatures. More than one trace, and she was only able to feel them because they were tight together. Like they had the same purpose.

And in their midst, a more familiar signal. But it was smothered. Either that, or it was guarding itself from detection.

Just like Cathal's lattice actively repelled her.

She focused, and sussed as tightly as she could. <*Tris, if you can hear me, respond. Are you okay?*>

He wasn't. And he didn't respond. But the hidden signal flared up, a brilliant burst that died as soon as it erupted, and Ryann thought of a hand thrust out by a drowning man.

"Ryann?" The word was drawn out, and Keelin was shaking, her hands clenched tight against her chest. The smile was far from her face now.

Ryann opened her arms, and the girl flung herself into them. She trembled as Ryann held her.

"It's going to be alright," she said. "We can't assume anything."

"You reached him?" The voice was muffled, and was followed by a sniff.

"Enough to know that he's still alive." But saying those words gave no comfort. If he was alive but unresponsive, what did that mean?

Ryann looked over to Cathal. "We can't assume anything," she repeated. "We can't jump to conclusions."

But that was exactly what Keelin would be doing. Ryann knew, because she was doing the same.

Keelin's body was warm, and Ryann squeezed. She didn't want to let go. She couldn't face losing anyone else.

Neither of them spoke. Keelin's trembling slowed. There was an occasional sniff.

It was important to grab these moments of calm, Ryann told herself.

Then Keelin pulled away, rubbing red eyes, and her warmth was replaced by a chill. Ryann didn't want to let her go. But she did.

"Sorry," the girl said, and looked down. She looked so young. And Ryann felt so old.

"Nothing to be sorry about." Ryann felt the words almost choke in her throat. She hadn't realised how close she'd been to tears, too. But that would be for later, in private. She had to stay strong. For Keelin.

The girl glanced up then, and her eyes were wide. But Ryann recognised the glazed look of someone sussing.

"Nyle," she said in explanation. "Half-way here. You want to talk?"

Ryann wondered if that was Keelin's suggestion, or Nyle's request. "Sure."

Keelin nodded, and Ryann felt the communication channel open, the trace of a new lattice fresh in her mind. The signal, like all Haven personnel, was in her records.

<This is Ryann Harris,> she sussed, keeping to full-name protocol before switching to something more informal. *<How's it going, Nyle?>*

<This storm's a bitch for flying, but it's nothing I can't handle. Hear you've got a bit of a problem. How you holding up?>

<Better for hearing you. How far out?>

<Should be with you in a couple of minutes. How do you want to play this? I understand you can't get out.>

<Not through the front.> Ryann thought, and looked over to Cathal, then to the rear door. *<But we'll get out. Land on the pad and light a path for us. Use all your arcs.>*

<Yeah, I've got that. Sol setting, right?>

<That's the one.>

<No problem. See you in a bit.>

Ryann cut communication, and Keelin looked at her with a quizzical expression.

"We can't go out there," she said. "Brice and Tris...we can't leave them. And we can't carry Cathal. Not through the hatch. We need the main door."

Ryann nodded slowly. They were fair points, and she had not ignored them. But she had to think about this logically. She had to consider what was right for the crew. Cathal's crew. Her crew.

She spoke as the thoughts formed in her mind, choosing her words with deliberation. "Keelin, we don't know what's happened to Tris and Brice. We do know they were on their way back, and if they're lost out there, we have a better chance of finding them with a Proteus." Yes, that made good sense. Keelin swallowed but dipped her head a couple of times. "And no, we can't head out the front. So we need to leave via the emergency hatch. All three of us."

She looked over to the blanket, so motionless that it was hard to imagine Cathal still breathed under there. While he had breath, he had life. But even if he didn't, he was her commander. He was a part of her crew. She could not leave Cathal behind.

He was her responsibility now.

"I'll carry him," she said. And that, finally, felt like the right decision.

Thirty-two

Brice walked on, because the only other option was to stop, and if he did that his legs would not want to move ever again.

The cold and the rain didn't register now. The burning of his muscles was a dull throb, constant and insistent. Sharp heat rose when branches scratched his arms and face, but the pain cooled as quickly as it rose.

The mud river was no more. Whether it sunk into the ground or turned off somewhere, Brice didn't know. He hadn't been watching. All he knew was that he was moving downhill, and that he was following some kind of path, little more than a trail of downtrodden ferns. He refused to think about what he was following.

His boot slipped on a root, and he gave a sharp cry as his ankle twisted. But that was more in surprise than anything else, and although it felt tender, it still held his weight. And he walked on.

He hadn't seen the root because he refused to use the torch. He told himself he'd save it for emergencies, conserving its power. Yet he knew he was fooling himself. The moment he heard or saw one of those things, it would be on him. He'd never have a hope of thumbing the control before those claws sliced through him.

If he had to die, he'd prefer it to be quick.

In the darkness, patterns shifted, and he chose to ignore them. A gap opened in the branches overhead, revealing bulbous, heavy clouds, and the forest around him became a shade lighter.

Everything was black and grey. He walked through a forest of shadows, alive with whispers and roars from the storm.

But that hiss, close to his ear, was not the wind or the rain. Brice was certain of that.

He stopped, his feet suddenly heavy. Hairs on his neck pushed against the congealed mud as they fought to stand erect. His skin tingled.

The hiss was close enough that he felt sickly warm air brush his face.

Brice turned, peering into the void.

Two orbs hovered at head height, dark shapes swirling within. Something glistened underneath them as lips parted to reveal dull fangs, grey against the black, and a blast of foetid breath washed over Brice.

The torch slipped from his hand, pulling at his wrist.

The creature hissed again, its head moving from side to side. Dark holes above its mouth twitched, like it was sniffing him out. It moved, unfolding from the branches. It stretched out with an arm, and claws dragged against the trunk of a tree. Brice saw water run along the scars they left. The creature's stink rolled over him.

He closed his eyes. The hiss swung left then right, and leaves moved. There was a snap from the ground as the creature stepped closer.

Brice swallowed, waiting for the end.

But the pain never came.

He opened his eyes, and already the shadow was moving away, along the track. It walked slowly, parting ferns with its hands, like it had all the time it cared to take. But it moved away from Brice. He watched its broad shoulders, and saw the ridge at the top of its spine, just at the base of its neck.

His own hand came up to his neck, fingers rubbing the grit against his skin. He missed the warmth of his lattice. He missed knowing what was going on with his body.

The creature was searching—that must be why it constantly moved its head from side to side—but it had missed Brice. He didn't understand how it could be so blind, but it gave him hope. Or maybe he was becoming delusional.

The creature was searching for food, maybe. The monsters had followed the crew from the cliff to the hold-out. They had followed Brice and Tris.

This beast was making for the hold-out.

Brice followed, on the verge of laughter. It was like a sheep following a wolf. Terrifying, but beyond ridiculous.

The creature increased its pace, forcing Brice to break into a run. He wondered if it knew Brice was following, and if it was trying to shake him off. But the monster never once looked back. It showed no signs of knowing Brice was there.

Soon, he could no longer see the beast, nor hear its movements. But he could still follow the path it took. And as he did so, he let his mind run free, because it was beginning to understand.

The creature had been close enough to kill Brice with one swipe of its claws, but it had ignored him. And back in the tunnels, the creature that attacked Cathal had then run straight into Brice. Almost like it didn't see him.

They existed in the dark, so they couldn't rely on sight. Hadn't Ryann suggested this? They'd use smell or—maybe because their own stench was too strong—sound. Or electrical impulses. He didn't understand science, but he knew these things would use something other than their eyes to 'see'.

And they didn't 'see' Brice.

As unlikely as that sounded, it explained so much. When the creatures had been swarming round Tris, they hadn't turned on Brice. And they infected the forest, yet Brice was able to walk with no protection.

He pushed against a branch, and it snapped, the crack echoing through the trees. He stopped, but nothing came for him. Maybe they couldn't hear, either.

The creature's path had disappeared, or maybe Brice had taken a wrong turn, because he was surrounded by trees and ferns and all the other plants he knew nothing about. But he could still feel the angle of the ground. He needed to keep moving downhill.

The undergrowth was thick, so Brice unsheathed one of his knives. He swung with an easy motion, left and down then right and up, using momentum and the turns of his body to do much of the work. It helped that he kept the blade sharp. The severed plants sprayed him with water, but they no longer barred his path, and he walked on, stronger than before. The movement in his arm sent warmth through his body, and he started to smile.

This was what he did. He moved. He used his body.

Light filtered through the trees, and that must have been lightning. The rumble of the thunder became more of a growl, like it was angry. And maybe it was—angry that, despite the muddy river and the rain and the cold, Brice still walked on. Angry that he was surviving everything it could throw at him.

Brice was a nothing, to the storm and to the creatures. And that meant he could slip through the cracks. That meant he had the advantage.

Up ahead, off to the left, Brice saw a flickering light through the moving trees. Then the area directly ahead began to glow, and the roar in the night sky changed into an angry whine.

Brice knew that sound. Usually, it was muffled, because he was inside. But when he connected to external sensors, this was the sound he heard—the deep whine of engines as a Proteus descended.

And he knew where the light came from.

With a cry, and a jump—an honest-to-goodness jump—for joy, he sprang forward, slashing his way to salvation.

Thirty-three

Ryann pulled her body close to the metal rungs. It made climbing awkward, but she had to leave room for Cathal. The emergency hatch wasn't designed for more than one person at a time.

Keelin had helped her bind Cathal to her back, just as she had done for Brice. His legs against her thighs felt strangely intimate, almost inappropriate, but they held him in place, and Ryann understood why Brice had wanted Cathal bound so tightly. Even his head at her shoulder—again, an intimacy that unsettled her—was practical.

At the top of the ladder, she spun the plate and pushed open the hatch. Water cascaded down, running into the hold-out and over her body. It dripped down her neck, running off Cathal's covered head. But it did nothing to wash away the stench.

Easing herself through the hatch felt to Ryann like a rebirth, from the concrete tomb to the welcoming embrace of nature, from the dark to the light. And it was light out here. The lantern attached to the relay bathed everything in wonderful sol.

The forest was alive. She could sense it as much as see it. The trees teemed with creatures, on the ground and higher up. They stayed back from the light, but only just. And when she pushed, Ryann sensed a cold desperation of purpose that drew them together.

"It's good to be out," Keelin said as she came through the hatch, and Ryann had to agree with her, despite the creatures. Keelin looked up, straining her eyes to see the dark beyond the light, and

Ryan followed her gaze, into the wide expanse of storm-clouds that cloaked the night sky.

Rain stung her eyes, and she blinked. But the moisture felt so invigorating.

"There!" Keelin pointed, and Ryann saw the glow in the clouds, and heard the growl of the Proteus' engines as the craft swung into view. It twisted in the storm, but slowly. Not cutting through the air, but riding it, forcing it into submission. And the air obeyed, buoying the shining object up, brushing the tree-tops and bending them with its down-draft.

<We've got visual, Nyle. Bring her down. I'll tell you when to open the hatch.>

<Sure thing. Your beacon works well. Thanks.>

Ryann smiled at that.

The Proteus came closer. Ryann pulled up filters to guard against the glare from the four arcs, over the main hatch. Nyle had them angled to cover as wide an area as possible, and Ryann wondered if this was his idea or Keelin's.

Under the craft, landing lights blazed with the same yellow luminosity. The beams blasted into the trees, and branches thrashed wildly. Shadows ran, and Ryann knew not all the movement was from down-draft.

The craft hovered over the landing pad. It spun, bringing the hatch side to face the ramp, and then it lowered. The light sunk beneath the trees.

"Come on," Ryann said, one hand on Keelin's shoulder. They jogged to the edge of the roof and strafed the treeline with their torches. Ryann saw movement and sensed…not panic, but uneasiness. Uncertainty.

"I'll go first," Keelin said, already lowering herself over the edge. She dropped, grunting as she landed on bended knees. After a glance up and a nod, Keelin stepped forward and aimed her beams at the trees.

Ryann let her torches dangle from her wrists as she sat on the edge as best she could, Cathal's bulk forcing her body into strange positions. She reached round, hands planted firmly, and then she twisted her body, clenching her arm muscles and pushing her boots into the concrete walls. Her weight spun lazily, and she had time to check the momentum, placing one boot wide to stop herself spinning too far.

She lowered herself until her arms were at full stretch, the toes of her boots flat on the wall, and the weight on her back pulling for the ground. Then she pushed with her feet and lifted her hands.

She hit the ground, and a bolt of pain erupted in her ankle. She threw her hands forward, and they scraped down the wet metal of the door, but they didn't stop her body tipping forward. They didn't prevent her crashing to the mud.

"Ryann!"

Torch-light shone in Ryann's face. "Watch the trees!" she said with a grimace, and Keelin turned the torch away.

<*You okay?*> the girl sussed.

<*Fine.*> And then Ryann twisted her body, ignoring the pain in her left leg. She reached out with one hand, used the door to steady herself, and stood. On her right foot.

Ahead was the ramp, and above that, on the landing pad, sat the Proteus. Its lights shone bright, but there were still shadows, and in the darkness Ryann saw shapes. They unfolded in the protection the landing pad offered.

"Keelin, we need to keep those things away from the ramp."

"On it." Keelin angled her shaking beams, and the creatures ran as their shadows burnt up, leaving an angry hiss in their wake. Then Keelin spun slowly, her feet shuffling and her arms waved wildly, covering as much of the treeline as possible.

Maybe, Ryann thought, the fear helped. Maybe the erratic movement of the lights worked in their favour.

But they needed to get to the Proteus. "Let's go," she said, and stepped forward.

White heat shot up from her left ankle, and she crashed to the ground. She heard Keelin yell.

<*Keep using the torches!*> Ryann rolled to one side, as far as Cathal would let her, and saw a dark shape moving. <*Behind you,*> she yelled at Keelin.

The girl spun as the creature raced from the trees, the height of the landing pad and the surrounding forest giving it a brief moment of protection. But Keelin brought her own beams up, and that protection dissolved. The creature staggered with an angry hiss, and collapsed in a tangle of limbs. But Keelin kept her torches aimed at the creature, the beams now tight and strong. The light grew hazy as steam rose from the creature's thrashing body.

And then it stopped moving. Its smoldering limbs curled uselessly around its lifeless, charred body.

Ryann waved her own torches in the other direction. The creatures held back, but she wasn't taking any chances.

<*Can you stand?*>

Ryann didn't want to answer. As soon as she'd felt the pain, she'd known what had happened. But she needed to carry Cathal to the Proteus. She couldn't leave him.

"I'll be fine." She pushed off from the ground, her weight on her good leg. She could feel the swelling in the other ankle. Not broken, but sprained.

She could force herself through the pain.

"I can carry him."

"No!" This was her burden. She was leading the crew. It was her fault anyway—if she'd sensed that third warth, or if she'd told Cathal of the traces in the tunnel, none of this would have happened. She couldn't pass this on to Keelin.

Ryann brought her own torches round, sending creatures darting back into the trees. They were becoming bolder. All it would take was a lapse of concentration, a brief moment where light did not surround Ryan and Keelin, and a creature could strike.

But Keelin was right—Ryann would never manage Cathal on her own.

"We'll do it between us," she said, and unfastened the straps around her chest.

<*You need a hand out there?*> Nyle called. He was aiming for nonchalant, but the fear and uncertainty were clear in his voice.

<*Keep where you are. Just open the hatch when we get close.*>

That should have been Ryann, but instead Keelin gave the command.

And it didn't matter, because they worked as a team.

The webbing came free, and Keelin moved to Ryann's side. Cathal's weight shifted as the girl put an arm round his back and, with a grunt, hoisted him up. Her free hand swept the torch round.

"Come on," she said.

Again, that should have been Ryann's line. But she couldn't think about talking. She needed to focus on walking.

Each step was agony. Ryann grimaced, forcing her lattice to stop the pain signals reaching her conscious mind, screaming at her body to ignore the damage and just cope, goddammit! She flashed her torch wildly, and the hisses from the trees washed over her, threatening to floor her with their rotten-meat stink. But she wouldn't fall. She couldn't let Cathal down.

They reached the bottom of the ramp. It was steeper than Ryann recalled, the surface slick with mud.

Keelin cried out, swinging her torch to force a creature back into the trees. But Ryann was certain it hesitated for a moment. Even as its hide started to bubble, it held its position.

Fighting the pain. Pushing itself forwards.

"Up!" she said, one word all she could manage before nausea gripped her.

<*Osker, you ready with the door?*> Keelin sussed.

<*Opening it now.*>

<*Grab a couple of torches. Aim them at anything that moves. Sol, maximum intensity.*>

<*On it.*>

Ryann looked up the ramp, to the brilliance above it. With filters in place, she could make out each of the four arcs, but she also saw two smaller beams that flew left and right. Osker, giving them safe passage.

They could do this. Only a short walk.

"Ready?" Keelin said. Ryann nodded. Flinching, she put pressure through her injured ankle and swung her right foot forward. It squelched into the mud, and she bent her knee and pushed, bringing her left leg round.

But when she placed that boot on the ground, the soil shifted, and her hand came forward, onto the mud, Cathal's weight rolled round.

"Again," Keelin said.

And again, they slipped back. Again, Ryann tasted bile at the back of her throat.

And the hiss of the creatures rose into a screech.

She sensed the movement behind her back, and felt a sickening hunger roll off the creatures. She saw Keelin stagger as she spun, bringing her beams round. Some of the screeching turned to cries of pain, and the stink of burning filled the air.

Ryann sunk to the mud until she was sitting. She waved her torches at the approaching shapes. And through the haze of steam and the glow of the light, she saw the creatures stagger as they shrieked. She saw how their skin ruptured, and how they jerked in pain. But she also saw how the creatures behind held them steady, using the burning bodies as shields.

And the angry hissing became a victory yell that clawed at the last of her hope, leaving Ryann with nothing to do but wait for the inevitable end.

THIRTY-FOUR

Brice ran, as fast as the forest would let him. He slashed through the undergrowth, throwing branches aside. He kicked forward, tripping on occasions, but always staggering on. Nothing was going to prevent him reaching that Proteus.

Light flickered through the tree-tops, and the whine of the craft's engines deepened. Brice knew what that meant—it was about to touch down. And it would have light, and warmth, and food. It would have a shower.

The arc lights—and for them to burn through the trees so powerfully, that must be what they were—cast shadows all around, swirling in the storm, the bark and the leaves glistening with the rain.

And Brice stopped. Because the shadows were alive.

The creatures moved, hiding from the light. Rain coated their hides, and their claws glinted where they curled around branches. As Brice stared, he saw more and more of them. They stood behind trunks, and they balanced way above him. They were close, and they were far away.

There were more than he could count.

Brice might be invisible to them, but they still blocked his path to the Proteus. When he'd tried getting through to Tris, they'd thrown him to one side. They'd do the same—or worse—now.

But they were focused on the Proteus. That might mean there were fewer around the hold-out.

Brice sheathed his knife and crept through the undergrowth, keeping parallel with the multitude of creatures. Through the trees he could see the torch he'd fixed to the relay. It gave him something to aim for.

The solid mass of concrete grew as a monolith, an immovable darkness amongst the thrashing forest. It reminded Brice of a tomb, the light on top showing respect for the recently departed. It was no longer a place of sanctuary, but a lifeless void.

He thought of Cathal, and of Keelin and Ryann, trapped within those walls. He pictured them collapsed, taken over by the stench from Cathal's wound. In his mind, their eyes were open but their chests were still.

And then he saw another light through the trees, part-way between the hold-out and the landing pad. A sharp cry of pain tore through the sibilance in the trees.

There were figures on the ramp. Two of them, with a third slumped between them. And then the figure closest to Brice slipped and fell.

Shadows crawled from the forest, filling the space between the ramp and the hold-out.

They pushed forward. The ones closest to the ramp smoked and burnt, but any that fell were held up by the ones behind.

Brice crept out, staying as far back as he could. He took a breath, and focused. The shadows swirled, but he saw limbs and heads, and they dissolved into individuals.

Four rows, about five creatures per row.

Twenty creatures. Any single one could take out a warth.

Had there been this many around Tris? He couldn't recall. But he could remember striking one of them on the back of the head. He could recall how it staggered.

They weren't invincible. Everything had a weak-spot.

And Brice was invisible.

His thumb stroked his last torch. He looked at the ramp. It was slippery with mud, but it wasn't as steep as the one by the other landing pad.

He breathed deep, stilling his mind, and looked. Really looked. He needed to take everything in. He saw where Cathal's blanket-bound body lay. He noticed how Ryann leaned in to Keelin, and how her left leg was stretched out more than her right. He saw how they each had two torches, and how Ryann moved hers smoothly while Keelin's jerked constantly. He noted which creatures were closest to death, and saw where others remained in the shadows.

He calculated distances. He visualised the movements his muscles must make.

He didn't make a decision. The situation dictated his actions.

Brice thumbed his torch to life. At the same time he screamed and ran.

He didn't know if the creatures heard him, or sensed him at all, because he was on them too quickly. Light flashed, but he concentrated on the shadows.

Brice swung an arm, and it jarred when it struck, and a creature staggered. But Brice was already moving forward, barrelling into another creature, barging it out of the way. He used this to ricochet to one side, swinging out with his torch now. Rancid breath washed over him, and he ducked, then pushed upwards, his fist ploughing forwards. He saw the neck of another creature, the one directly in front of him, and he brought his fist down, as hard as he could.

The creature staggered and fell, tripping over the burning shield that slipped from its grasp.

The air tasted of overcooked flesh and decay, but also of sweat and adrenaline.

Brice saw the shape on the ground as he stepped onto the ramp. He dipped down, powering his legs forward at the same time. His body was off-balanced for a moment, but that was fine. That was what Brice wanted. He needed the momentum.

His hands pushed through the mud, and he scooped Cathal up. He tipped forward, but his left leg was ready, his boot slamming into the mud as his thigh pushed. Cathal rose, and Brice threw his right leg forward, bringing his knee up under Cathal's body.

“I’ve got him,” he managed to shout at an open-mouthed Keelin. “You help Ryann.”

The blankets covering Cathal flapped against his legs with each powered thrust. Brice didn’t stop. He couldn’t. As soon as one boot came down, the other one rose. Even as his feet slipped back, he took another step, and another, and he gained ground. He gripped Cathal tight to his chest, ignoring the stench from his wound, ignoring the burn in his arms. He looked to the light that grew brighter with each step.

When he reached the end of the ramp, and his feet stopped sliding back, he turned. Ryann and Keelin were near the top, seated in the mud, pushing themselves backwards. That gave them the freedom of both hands, and four torch beams slashed across the creatures at the bottom of the ramp. The air was hazy, and the shrieks drowned out the storm.

Brice twisted his arm so that his torch joined theirs. They reached the top of the ramp and stood, supporting each other. No—Keelin supporting Ryann.

“Go! Get in the Proteus!”

Keelin nodded. They ran with a hopping gait, and Ryann cried out with every step. But they didn’t stop.

Brice ran by their side, Cathal tight to his chest, the blankets flailing. Brice squinted into the light, and maybe he saw an open hatch below the arcs. There was a shadow, and for a moment Brice thought the creatures were ahead of them. But this shadow danced with a couple of beams of light, and Brice knew it was a person.

And he recognised the stance, and the way the man moved.

Osker. Another grunt. Given the job of opening the hatch, while the rest of the crew sat inside in comfort.

Brice staggered, and Osker called out, something about hurrying up. But his voice was lost in the roar of the Proteus, and the deep boom of thunder that erupted suddenly, almost at the same moment the sky burst open.

Something caught under Brice’s foot, and Cathal’s weight lunged forwards. Brice held him tight, his body twisting. He hit the ground hard and rolled over, away from the bundle of blankets.

A voice yelled out a name.

The light was too bright, and Brice squinted again, shielding his eyes with an arm. He saw the blanket, and there was a hand protruding. As Brice watched, the skin started to bubble and blister.

He reached over, grabbing a corner of the blanket and throwing it over the hand, covering Cathal's exposed flesh.

An animal shriek ripped through his head. Brice spun, pushing his feet under his body, and brought his torch round. A shape flew from the trees and landed on the landing pad. It crouched, then straightened up, arms outstretched.

Brice stood and yelled, taking a step forward. He aimed his beam at the beast's head, and the orbs were lost in the brilliance. The creature writhed, arms flailing. It took a step back, and fell from the landing pad.

But others were jumping now. He saw them leave the trees and throw themselves onto the landing pad.

It was suicide, but only for the first to be struck by the light. The others used the smoldering bodies as shields, as they had done at the bottom of the ramp.

And the trees writhed.

A voice yelled warm breath into Brice's ear. He turned. Keelin. She grabbed his arm and pulled, yelling again for him to get inside.

Her eyes darted behind him, and he instinctively swung his torch round, ducking at the same time. The claw sliced the air in front of his face, and the creature's fangs shone in the torch-light. It staggered, and Brice kicked out, as hard as he could. The thing fell, Keelin's torchlight joining his as the creature writhed under a growing mist.

The cloying stink of burning flesh had never tasted so good.

"Come on!" Keelin yelled once more, and she pulled him away.

"Cathal!" he yelled, eyes darting around, trying to find the man.

"Osker's got him." Keelin pulled once more, then set off at a run. Brice looked up, and through the light he saw Oskar, out of the hatch, dragging a body. He had his hands under Cathal's armpits, and he looked like he was about to throw up.

But he was the grunt. He did what was needed.

Brice ran after Keelin. He trod on cloth, and realised Cathal was unprotected.

"Get him covered!" he yelled, knowing nobody would hear. The growl from the Proteus' engines increased as it prepared to pull away. Brice looked above the hatch, to the four arc-lights.

And there were shadows in the spaces between the arcs.

Through the pounding of the rain he heard creatures landing on metal.

"Get inside!" he yelled to Keelin. Ryann, already in the doorway, dragged Cathal in as Osker turned, waving his torches around.

And then one of the shadows dropped.

The creature grabbed Osker tightly, covering him like a shroud. It dipped its head, and Brice knew he saw fangs. Then Osker cried out, and something erupted from his neck.

The creature lifted its head, its skin bubbling, and red drool dripped from its mouth. It pulled Osker's head to one side, opening the wound to an obscene angle. It lowered its mouth once more, Osker's blood spraying into its throat.

Then it uttered a high-pitched scream as it threw its arms up and staggered back. Osker collapsed to the floor of the hatch, and Brice saw Keelin behind him, two torches held straight in front of her. She stepped towards the creature, and it jerked back. Its legs buckled and it fell, the scream fading.

Keelin took a step and kicked, sending the smoldering remains flying to the mud, and then she staggered, grabbing the Proteus. Brice bounded forward, arms open. He grabbed her, and his momentum carried them both into the craft.

They crashed to the ground, and Brice felt the Proteus shudder. The hatch door whined, high-pitched against the boom of the engines, and started to seal.

There was a thud from above. He looked up to see an arm reaching down, between the arc lights. Claws flexed, and the arm extended. But it was already too late. The hatch locked into place with a clunk. The limb hung for a while before falling to the floor.

There was no blood.

Keelin looked away, and Brice only now realised he held her tight, and she had her arms around him too. He couldn't tell which of them was shaking. And on the floor beside them, in a slowly spreading dark pool, was a bloody mess that had once been Osker.

Off to one side lay Cathal, with Ryann by his side. She had a hand under the single blanket that covered his body. Her head was down and her eyes closed. She looked ready to collapse.

But it was over. They were safe.

Keelin pulled away from him, and stood. He watched her chest rise and fall as she took in deep breaths, and her mouth opened and closed wordlessly. She didn't meet his eyes. Then she looked through the door and into the bridge.

"Nyle, get us the hell out of here," she choked.

Brice just wanted to close his eyes and sleep.

THIRTY-FIVE

But Brice didn't close his eyes. He watched Keelin leave the cabin. She didn't look back.

"Brice, do something with this mess."

He turned to Ryann, but her attention was on Cathal, one hand under the blanket and the other on his forehead. Brice looked to the floor, from Cathal to Osker to the severed arm to the general untidiness of the whole place.

"Specifics?" he asked. He didn't have the energy to use any more words.

"Cover Osker. Remove the arm. Tidy the place up a bit." She tilted her head. "It's not an order. Just a request. Please."

She sounded disinterested, or maybe wary. But then her head turned from Cathal. "But don't bother with the stores," she said, firmly.

"Okay." That seemed strange, but he didn't want to go near the stores anyway. Units were open, clothing lay in untidy piles, and mugs adorned the table-top. In one of the storage units he saw an old blanket, muddy and rancid. Brice didn't want to think about what might be under it.

He guessed the commander of this Proteus wasn't as fastidious as Cathal.

There were cleaning supplies under the food prep area. He grabbed what he needed and set to work. At least it gave him something to do. It wasn't as if Ryann was providing much in the way of conversation, and the door to the bridge was closed now. He might as well have been on his own.

He tried not to look at Osker, but those open, unmoving eyes seemed to follow Brice around the cabin. Every time he turned, he expected Osker to have moved.

Brice knew he was being ridiculous. The man was dead. He repeated that to himself, every time he saw the pool of blood and the gaping wound in his throat. The man was no longer alive, and there was nothing Brice could do about that. He'd watched the beast rip Osker's flesh. He'd seen the look of horror on the man's face as, surely, he realised this was the end.

He'd come to rescue Brice and the others, and he'd lost his life. He'd died following orders. He'd never see Haven again.

"Here," Ryann said, and when Brice looked up she seemed distant and blurred. Everything did. She held a cloth out to him. He took it and wiped the moisture from his face. Maybe that was nothing but the rain.

"You okay?" she asked.

"Probably not," he said, because it was easier to be honest. "But I'll get my work done." He tried to smile, and the muscles in his face felt stiff.

"Thank you." Ryann managed a small smile, out of character but so very welcome. The hand under the blanket moved, like she was gently patting Cathal.

"How is he?" Brice asked.

"Alive." Her voice was small, and she didn't elaborate.

Brice moved to Osker, wrapping him in a sterile body-wrap. He never thought he'd have to do this for real. Training felt like a game now, or maybe a competition. It didn't mean anything.

He moved the body—the person—carefully to one side, doing what he could to secure it—him—in place. Then he mopped, swirling red into pink, spreading the discoloured patch across the floor. The mop became dirty and congealed, and Brice wanted to open the hatch and throw it out.

Brice turned to the creature's severed arm. He expected the leathery feel, but he wasn't prepared for the coldness, not so soon after it had been removed from the body. He was sure there should be some residual warmth.

The floor around Osker—and Brice forced himself to think the man's name, as painful as it was—had been blood-soaked, sticky and rich with a sickening coppery tang. But around the arm there was only a thin dribble of moisture, slightly viscous where he swirled it with his boot.

"They don't bleed," he said, more to push back the quiet than anything else.

"Apparently not." Ryann was watching him now. "At least, not all the time."

"And daylight kills them." Brice recalled the charred remains of the one that had killed Osker. It was right that the beast had died for what it had done.

"They are…strange. Most interesting."

Ryann's tone was flat. She bent over the infected body of Cathal, yet she was acting like the creatures that had done this to him were to be studied rather than to be despised.

Maybe that was her way of coping.

Brice turned away, and looked to the corner of the cabin, by the hatch. He counted five torches in a pile, and only now realised that his own had gone, because it no longer dangled from his wrist. He didn't even know if it was one of those five or not.

A couple of others rolled around the floor. He added them to the pile. They looked untidy, and he considered putting them away. But Ryann had told him to steer clear of the storage units.

"You finished?" Ryann said. Brice nodded, noticing how she, too, had been looking to the stores. "You want to go up front with the others?"

"You okay here on your own?" He knew she wasn't making a suggestion, but it seemed wrong to leave.

"I'm not alone," she said, her eyes now back on the blankets.

"Okay." He supposed she was right. And if she wanted company she could always suss.

Brice took another look around the cabin. It felt familiar, yet so different to their own Proteus. Cathal would never have allowed Keelin's baby to get in such a state. The mugs would have been cleaned straight after use, and clothes would have been stowed. And he definitely wouldn't have allowed that blanket to stink the place up. It looked like it had been used to clean the floor, or like it had been dragged around outside.

With a lump in his throat, Brice made his way to the bridge, sealing the door behind him.

"Brice," said the man in the pilot seat, and his face was familiar when he turned, although Brice recalled it with more colour.

"Nyle. Thanks." What else could he say?

"Osker…you've taken care of him?"

When Keelin put a hand on the pilot's arm, Brice expected Nyle to break down. But he took a deep breath and held Brice's gaze.

"I've taken care of him," Brice said. "At least the thing that did it to him is gone."

"There is that."

Nyle's head shifted towards Keelin, and Brice knew they were sussing. And he realised how Nyle and Osker would have been in contact. Although Nyle had been in the bridge, he would've known what was happening outside.

He would've been with Osker as the man died. Another helpless observer. Another victim, simply following Kaiahive's orders.

"How are you doing, Brice?" Keelin asked. He nodded, because he didn't really know.

The Proteus shuddered and the light flickered.

"Storm's not letting up," Nyle said, then looked up. "At least it helped wash those things off the roof."

Brice thought of the severed arm. "None up there now?" he asked.

"Some hung on for a while, but I guess it was too slippery." Nyle's voice was a monotone

"Slippery everywhere in this weather," Brice said, remembering the river of mud, and the landing pad ramps. He remembered how he'd staggered while carrying Cathal, and how the blanket got caught round his feet.

And now he remembered Osker dragging Cathal into the Proteus, and how Cathal's skin had been burning in the light.

The blankets were standard issue, from the hold-out. But a Proteus was a crew's home-from-home. The quarters were personalised. Keelin had her red-lined fleece topper. Ryann had her brilliant white bedding.

None of them had a blanket that looked as grey and nondescript as the two on Cathal. Correction—the one on Cathal.

And the one on this Proteus. The one in the overflowing storage space. The blanket that looked like it had been soaking in mud. Or something worse.

The room spun, and Brice grabbed the back of Keelin's chair.

"What is it?" she said.

Brice turned to the door of the bridge. He swallowed.

"We didn't get rid of them all," he said.

Thirty-six

Ryann knew they were not alone. As soon as Nyle got them airborne, and the creatures clinging to the hull had fallen, a single trace remained.

She didn't believe it would attack while the lights were on sol. She'd sussed Nyle, telling him to keep that setting, at least for the moment. She said it was a comfort.

She knew he didn't believe her. But, even though this was his craft, she outranked him. He could question her, but he couldn't deny her request. Especially not when her crew outnumbered his.

She hated the coldness of that thought. Lives should never be reduced to simple numbers. Besides, she didn't even know the numbers for her own crew. Cathal was alive, but for how much longer? And Tris—until she knew for certain, he was in limbo.

She had not asked Brice what happened, and her lack of knowledge, her lack of understanding, left a hollowness inside. But how could she expect him to talk, after everything that had happened? He'd been running on nervous energy the whole time he cleaned, and she'd only kept him at those tasks because he needed time. He needed to work the adrenaline from his system.

But she wanted him out of the way as quickly as possible. There had been too many casualties already—not only Tris missing, but Osker too. She didn't want to lose anyone else. She needed Keelin, Brice and Nyle to be safe.

So when Brice finished tidying, and when he sealed the door to the bridge behind him, she smiled. Because finally she was alone. Only herself and Cathal.

And the creature hiding under the blanket.

It hadn't moved yet, but she could sense it waiting. There was a taste of uncertainty, but no fear.

Of course it didn't fear Ryann. Remove the protecting light, and she was weak. The creature was powerful. Its claws could tear her flesh. Its fangs could rip her to pieces. It was a thing devoid of life, little more than a machine.

But it had life once. If Arela's hints were true, that thing had been a person. Like Cathal. But the company had treated it like an object, and had turned it into something damned.

It would be a blessing for that poor creature if she could end its suffering.

And she knew how this could happen. She could open the hatch, using her position to override any fail-safes Nyle had in place. She could coax it to the edge, and she could push it out. Or she could grab it and jump.

Her face pulled tight, her mouth parched and her throat tight. The thought of throwing herself from the Proteus went against everything she held dear.

Yet it made perfect sense. Safety and survival of the majority. If she were to go—to die—while removing that thing, then four people returned to Haven. If she didn't try, maybe none of them would make it.

<Ryann?> Keelin sussed, her voice unsteady. *<You alone back there?>*

<Just me and Cathal.> Strange how easy it was to lie at a time like this. Maybe because she wanted Keelin out of her head. She needed to be alone. *<Why?>*

<Brice thinks we've got company.> The tremor in Keelin's voice was unmistakable.

Brice didn't think, he knew. She'd seen the way he glanced at the blanket, hadn't she? He was smart enough to have figured things out.

<I'm fine,> she sussed back. That wasn't a total lie. Compared to how she could be, she was in great shape.

The Proteus lurched, and the lighting flickered. Ryann told herself it was nothing to worry about. Just the storm, and a patch of turbulence. Nyle had been through a lot. She couldn't expect a smooth ride home.

And the blanket moved.

It unfolded out of the storage unit and glided towards the centre of the room. Patches of the cloth were dark and wet, and Ryann could smell the earthy mustiness of it, and beneath that the rancid stench of the creature itself.

The same smell that came from Cathal's wound. Her hand pressed down on him, sensitive to the soft rise and fall of his chest.

The creature must be crouching, she realised. At full height, the blanket would be almost on the ceiling. But that would leave its lower legs exposed. It was keeping itself covered.

How had it figured out to use the blanket for protection? Had it seen how they covered Cathal? Or was it an old memory, from when…from before it became what it now was?

The blanket stretched forward, as if the creature wanted a closer look at Ryann. She heard snuffling, like it was sniffing her out.

But it didn't attack.

<Ryann?>

She wanted to tell Keelin to keep quiet. She needed to concentrate.

<Is everything okay?>

The girl wasn't going to let her be.

<I'm not alone.>

<What's it doing?> There was no hesitation. Keelin knew about the creature.

<Watching me.>

She reached out with her lattice, focusing on the trace. She tasted its interest, and also its hunger, and sensed the struggle between the two. And it responded to her probing, pushing back.

At the same time, she pushed into Cathal. His lattice still

repelled her, but now there was a spark from deep within, and she felt energy flowing. She sensed…not a normal sussuration, but something similar, and it reached out. Through her.

The creature pushed through Ryann too. As if she were nothing but a conduit.

Ryann focused tight, cutting out Keelin, and directed her energy towards the creature.

<*Who were you?*> she asked.

Then the lights flickered again, and the brief moment of dark pulled her back into the cabin. Or maybe it was the way the creature jerked.

The yellow glow returned, and the creature settled down.

Ryann's body tingled, and her head throbbed. Pushing like this, especially into the unknown, was always a struggle. She needed a moment to recover. She could do without interruptions.

<*You having issues with power, Nyle?*> she asked.

<*Been doing that since we took off. I'm doing my best.*>

<*Appreciate it. Keelin, you able to help him?*>

<*I'll do what I can, but…What do you want to do, Ryann?*>

How could Ryann respond to that? There was no way she could tell the girl that she intended to throw both herself and the creature from the craft.

<*Not sure,*> she sussed. <*Just keep the power flowing. As long as we've got sol, we're safe.*>

But Ryann didn't believe that now. At the landing pad, the creatures had pushed into the light. In the confined space of this cabin, the creature could easily strike out. It might even manage that while still covered with the blanket.

Ryann glanced at the pile of torches in the corner. Maybe if she could shine one up under the blanket, she'd have a chance. If she was quick.

But she'd never be quick enough. The creature would be on her before she'd even thumbed the controls.

The door to the bridge slid open, and Brice stepped through, followed by Keelin. The door sealed behind them.

<*What the hell are you doing?*> The words came out before Ryann could stop them.

<*Brice has an idea.*> Keelin sussed. Her wide eyes never left the blanket.

<*No. Whatever it is. Get out. I'll deal with this.*>

<*He thinks he can pull the blanket off.*>

<*No!*>

The creature was fast. Even if Brice managed to pull the blanket, the creature would attack. In such a small space, those claws could reach both Brice and Keelin.

She couldn't allow any more suffering. She had to protect her crew.

<*I won't allow it. Get back to the bridge.*>

But it was too late. The blanket swayed as the creature turned towards the door.

THIRTY-SEVEN

The whole cabin stank. Rotten meat, decay and blood. Brice kept his lips firmly closed, and still it stuck to the back of his throat.

Ryann was where Brice had left her, sat next to Cathal. She had one hand under the blanket and the other raised in the air. Not to ward off the creature, but with her palm towards Brice and Keelin.

But he wasn't going anywhere. He wasn't going to let that thing win.

It was facing him now. He could tell by the way the blanket moved, and by the bulge as it raised an arm. Almost like it, too, was telling them to get back.

He wasn't going to accept that from Ryann, and he sure as hell wasn't going to let some monster order him around.

Brice took a step forward. He told himself the tremble in his legs was from being cold and wet. His hand fell to his waist, and brushed against his lash. Useless, he knew, and he moved his hand further round. His fingers curled round the handle of a knife. He swallowed. The back of his neck itched.

The creature came a half-step closer. Brice caught a muffled hiss, and foul air washed over him.

Keelin shuffled to the side, and the blanket moved, as if the creature was watching her. She trembled, and took another step away from the door, her back against the wall.

Brice forced himself to side-step in the opposite direction. He didn't want to leave Keelin so exposed, but what else could he do?

Even if he stood directly in front of her, the creature could reach whoever it wanted. There was nothing he could do except remove the blanket.

And the only way he'd get close enough was if the creature was distracted.

His fingers twitched, no longer balled into fists. He stretched them, and pictured how they'd grab the crease in the blanket, up near the monster's head.

Ryann hadn't moved her body, but her head twitched, and Brice knew she was sussing.

The light flickered again. Brice swallowed, his throat dry.

The creature inched closer to Keelin, and she froze. A gasp escaped her mouth before she slammed her lips tight. Her brow glistened with sweat.

Brice stepped forward and brought his arm up.

And the blanket twitched. It spun as the door to the bridge slid open.

"What the hell are these things?"

Nyle stood in the open doorway, lash held high.

The lights flickered, then dimmed. Everything turned grey, and Brice saw the blanket rise up as the creature stretched.

"Nyle, get back and sort these damned lights out!" Brice said through clenched teeth.

The top of the blanket leaned in, and the creature sniffed.

"They killed Osker!"

Brice had no time to yell a warning as Nyle squeezed the trigger. The blanket rippled where the bolt of energy struck it.

But it didn't move backwards. Instead, it rose higher. Brice took the scene in, even though it only lasted a fraction of a second. Dark feet emerged from the shadows, toes ending in hardened tips that curled over. Muscle rippled in the creature's ankles.

Nyle screamed, and raised his lash again. Keelin yelled a half-strangled "No!", and held one hand out, but another bolt struck the blanket.

The creature shrieked, sharp and angry. And then it jumped.

It bounded to the wall, between Keelin and Nyle. A black arm flew from the blanket, and struck Keelin across her face. She cried out as she spun, slamming into the wall and crashing to the floor.

The creature lifted the blanket high, exposing itself to the dim light. Its fangs glistened as it gave a victory cry and flung itself at Nyle, its claws digging into his back as the creature pulled him close. The blanket fell, covering the two of them as the beast held Nyle in that awful embrace.

The cloth did nothing to muffle the screams. Brice heard the crack of the lash once more, and then it dropped, and a foot kicked it away, as useless as it had always been. The blanket writhed, bulging out in all directions at one. Then it slid and fell to the ground.

The creature's mouth was tight around Nyle's neck, catching the arc of blood. In the grey half-light, Brice saw dark patches leaking between its fangs, and as Nyle's scream faded out the slurping sound increased.

Then the creature pulled its head away, letting a few drops of crimson spill to the ground. It stood, and threw Nyle's body aside. His eyes were shut. He didn't move. Brice couldn't tell if he was alive or dead.

The wound on his neck looked like the one Cathal had, only red and raw.

The creature rose to its full height, its head almost touching the overhead light that was no longer a threat. Dark moisture oozed from its mouth, the lips drawn back in a snarl. Then it tilted its head back, brought its arms out, and let loose a cry that was both pleasure and victory.

Only not to Brice. To Brice, it sounded like a death sentence.

The creature spun, hissing angrily, and stepped towards Ryann and Cathal. She had a hand stretched towards the torches, and it trembled as she watched the creature. But she carried on moving, and the hand that remained on Cathal started to slide towards the edge of his blanket.

The creature leaned in, and the sound it made was guttural and cracked, and full of menace.

Ryann froze.

Then she eased away from the torches, and her hand slid back beneath the blanket.

The creature backed off. Its head dipped in a grotesque parody of a nod.

Brice turned his head to Keelin. She stared wide-eyed at the creature, and Brice could hear her breathing, fast and shallow.

Yet he felt calm. His heart hammered in his chest, but his own breaths were slow and steady. And he was able to think clearly.

The creature had the advantage, but only because the light had changed. They needed to switch it to sol. Nyle couldn't do that, but Keelin was a pilot. The Proteus would allow her to take control.

He caught her eye. He nodded his head to the door, then raised his eyes to the ceiling, hoping that she understood.

She looked to the door, then dropped her gaze. Brice followed it, to where Nyle lay in the doorway.

But Keelin didn't have a choice. She'd have to step over him.

Brice signalled with his head again, to the bridge and to the ceiling.

Keelin nodded. She took a deeper breath, then started to shuffle. Her eyes darted between the door, Nyle, and the creature.

It remained in the middle of the room, as still as a statue. Brice could only see its back, but he knew it was focused on Ryann. And she stared up at it, like she was transfixed. Her lips were separated, and they twitched, as if she were trying to talk.

Keelin was close to Nyle now, and Brice saw her shudder. She whimpered.

Ryann's eyes flashed towards the door.

The creature spun. It growled as it hunched over, arms out wide, claws clacking as its digits flexed.

Brice felt the knife at his side, and wondered when he'd unsheathed it. He stared at the beast's rolling shoulders, and the bulge at the base of its neck.

He brought his free hand up to his own neck, rubbing the skin. And he remembered swinging a torch. He remembered it striking a creature's neck.

Keelin's eyes darted from the creature to the open door, her head unmoving. But Brice saw the way she held the rest of her body. He knew what she was preparing for.

And he knew how the creature would react.

She'd never get there in time.

Not unless he helped.

Keelin took one last look at the creature. Sweat beaded over her eyes. And then she ran.

Brice launched himself the instant she moved, and the creature lunged at the same moment. Brice threw his arms forward, and he grabbed cold, hard leather. He squeezed his fingers and pulled.

The creature stank, but Brice gripped tighter. The hiss became a wail, close enough to Brice's ears that he felt the icy air shudder. Then he flung his other arm around the creature's chest, keeping a vice-like grip on the knife.

The creature flailed. It spun, lifting Brice from the floor. He squeezed himself as close to the beast as he could. Clung to it like it had held Nyle.

Pain slammed along his spine as the creature threw itself back against a wall, and stars burst in Brice's eyes. But the movement forced Brice closer. He shifted his grip, his fingers digging into the flesh under the creature's armpit.

The stench burnt his nose. He swallowed vomit.

Claws raked across his arm, tearing his jacket, as the creature reached behind itself. It jerked forward, then slammed back, and once more Brice hammered into the wall. But the creature twisted at the last moment, and Brice slipped. He only held on with one white-knuckled hand.

The beast spun again, screaming, and a brilliant light flashed in Brice's eyes. The stink of burning flesh hit him, and the creature twisted violently. Where Brice still grabbed the thing, under its arm, he pushed in with his fingers, and flesh rolled and bubbled, like it was alive.

Bright yellow beams cut through the air, and Ryann yelled in anger.

The creature lurched, and Brice's boots struck the floor. The beast dragged him. Not away from the light, but towards it. Brice was thrown to one side as the creature thrust an arm round, and the beams of light flew away. Brice saw Ryann fall into a corner. She landed in the pile of torches, sending them skittering across the floor.

Brice's fingers were white-hot, and he could not hold on much longer. He scrambled his feet, and then pushed with his legs. As the creature turned, Brice swung his free arm.

Something metal flashed.

His knife.

The creature swung its arm again, but Brice was ready this time. He used the momentum, twisting with the creature. He screamed as he powered his arm down, his vision filled with the back of the creature's neck.

It wailed, far louder than Brice believed could be possible. It spun violently, and Brice no longer had a grip on anything. He crashed down hard, and the air exploded out of his lungs.

The creature writhed, staggering on its feet. It crashed into the storage units, and bellowed even louder. It twisted its arms round, trying to reach behind its head.

Trying to grab the knife stuck hilt-deep in its neck.

Light burst into Brice's vision, and Ryann was standing, a torch in each hand. The beams of light criss-crossed the room, following the frenzied creature.

"Get more torches!" she yelled.

There were a couple close by, and Brice grabbed them. He rose, swaying, to his feet, and thumbed the torch controls. He ignored the pain tearing down his arm, and the tightness in his chest. He ignored everything but the creature and the wonderful sol light.

The beast fell and rolled onto its back. Brice aimed a beam at the thing's face, into those cold orbs. The creature buckled, legs kicking out and arms flailing. The stench of burning rose in steam, the mass of movement sending it up in angry bursts that hit Brice. It made his eyes water and his throat itch. But he kept the beams of light steady. He held them trained on the creature, sol eating away at its flesh.

Then the flailing became twitching, and the creature pulled its arms in tight to its chest. It curled into a foetal ball. Where the light hit its back, blisters popped, spraying translucent liquid in a fine mist that mixed with the steam. There was no blood, but the creature's hide ran semi-fluid now, oozing towards the floor.

And then the screaming stopped, and the blackened mass of the creature lay still.

Only then did Brice give in to his body's demands, and allow himself to collapse.

THIRTY-EIGHT

The smell reminded Ryann of her parents' farm, when they had to get rid of diseased animals. She'd cried then, too, even though she knew it needed to be done.

The torches were heavy in her hands, and she placed them by her feet. She made sure they were powered down first, though. It was important to do things properly.

Then, and only then, did she take in the room. It was important to analyse any situation as soon as the adrenaline began to fade.

She recorded, unwilling to fully trust her memory. She pulled up filters, and saw heat swirl in the room. The source was the charred mess, although it was already cooling, and a dark residue spread out beneath it. Like burning plastic, she thought, like something unreal.

Brice sat next to the remains, his head in his hands but his breathing steady. Blood coated a sleeve of his jacket, pooling and dripping from the elbow.

She didn't even try to reach his lattice, and it struck her just what he had achieved. Dark, without enhancements, yet he had taken on one of the creatures. And he'd survived. Ryan felt both humbled and proud.

Cathal always said the lad had potential.

"You okay?" she asked, and he turned to her, his face drained of emotion. But he nodded, and that was enough. He appeared younger, but maybe that was down to the way the light in the room suddenly grew brighter.

<*Keelin?*> Ryan called.

<*Here.*>

<*You got control of the Proteus then?*>

<*Thought it best. Letting it run on auto while I fix the power.*> Her words were cheerful, but her tone was worn out, and Ryann imagined the smile on the girl's face would be painful to hold.

<*Any joy?*>

<*Think I can see the problem. I'll keep you informed.*>

That would keep Keelin occupied. If she had a focus, she wouldn't dwell on what they'd been through.

<*Thanks.*>

Ryann looked through the open door to the bridge, but from this angle she couldn't see the pilot's position. But she did see Nyle's body, blocking the doorway.

She reached out for him as her eyes examined the wound, so like Cathal's.

"Brice, grab a medi-kit." She knelt beside the pilot, pressing a hand to the back of his neck to forge a stronger connection. He was warm, and energy coursed through his lattice. She had expected that.

"Here." Brice placed the medi-kit down and crouched next to her. She noted the grunt of exhaustion as he did so. "Anything I can do?"

She took a breath. He'd done so much already.

"Syringe," she said. "Labelled 'Cleanse A-6'. Then I'll need a pad. Largest you can find. Thanks."

She heard him rummaging through the kit, and she thought back to when she'd treated Cathal's wound in the cave. Only a few hours ago, yet it felt like an age had passed. She was older now, wearied yet wiser.

Brice handed her the needle-less syringe, and she readied it, knowing what was to come. She cleaned his wound, letting his limbs flail, knowing the spasms would pass. As she placed the pad over his wound, fastening it with the sealing strips, she imagined his skin changing, and his whole body becoming something else. She breathed in the trace of the aroma that would grow stronger as the disease took control of his body.

They'd have to find a blanket to cover him soon, to protect him from the light.

"He going to be okay?" Brice asked.

Ryann nodded, even though she wasn't sure. He'd live, if becoming one of those things could be called living.

"Not Osker, though." There was an edge of anger in Brice's voice—not the petty rivalry she was used to, but something more deep-seated. She turned to face him, automatically clearing up the detritus of her medical administrations as she did so. Brice didn't meet her gaze, but looked to the corner, where Osker lay in his body-bag.

"That couldn't be helped," she said. "There were too many creatures. You know that."

"But he didn't deserve to die. He was just doing his job." Brice spoke quietly, through clenched teeth. "He was only doing what he was told to do."

"That's all any of us do," Ryann said, although she didn't really believe that now. It was only what they did when they were too weak to think for themselves.

Brice huffed. "Sure. We do what the company tell us to. And look where it gets us." His mouth opened, as if he had more to say, but the words never came.

Ryann nodded, and it shocked her to realise she shared his bitterness.

The company had never been perfect. It was too big for that, and there would always be issues. There would always be paper-pushers who didn't understand, who cut corners to boost profits.

But since that conversation with Arela, hidden resentments had risen within Ryann, grasping hold of new facts. Where before she felt annoyance, now she loathed the company.

She looked to the remains of the creature, to what Kaiahive—and how she hated that name now—had created and then abandoned. And she wondered what would happen to those the beasts had infected. Would the company abandon Cathal and Nyle too?

She no longer wanted to work for such monsters.

Brice stood, and walked towards the creature. “We want to get rid of this thing?” He kicked it, his boot squelching into its body, and that made Ryann feel nauseous. “Open the hatch, chuck it out? Might clear the air a bit.”

She could understand his anger. She knew how he was channelling all his hatred onto those remains. The creatures had killed Osker. They had taken Tris, and left Cathal and Nyle in a state of limbo. They had put Brice through hell.

But it had been a person. Once, it had been just like them. She couldn’t hate it because of what others had done.

“No,” she said softly, and he turned to her in surprise. She thought fast. “We need to understand them. We need to learn whatever we can.” But she didn’t add that the creature was as much a victim as they were, and it deserved their respect.

Brice’s fists clenched and unclenched, and his chest rose as he took a deep breath. Then he stepped away, holding his injured arm close to his body. She’d have to see to that soon.

“This isn’t over, is it?” he said, his eyes still on the remains of the creature.

She shook her head. This was only just the start.

But for now, their night was over. They had a reprieve, and a chance to finally rest.

Ryann closed her eyes for a second. When she opened them, the cabin was flooded with a soft, beautiful yellow glow.

She looked through to the cabin. Keelin had turned in her seat, a grin on her face.

“We have power,” she said. And Ryann had to swallow to stop the tears from falling.

“The Proteus still on auto?”

Keelin shook her head. “I’ve taken control. Feels a bit strange, but it’s good to be flying again. You want me to set a course?”

Ryann did. A part of her wanted to tell Keelin to turn the craft around and head out of the basin, over the rim, and as far from this mess as possible. But she knew where they needed to go.

"Haven," she said. Even though that meant returning to Kaiahive, it also meant returning to Arela, and the other crews, and everything that was good about the place. "Take us home."

The creature watched from the high branches. As the craft retreated into the sky, and that burning light fled, it emerged, focusing on the aftermath.

It sensed the burning from below, and knew what blood remaining in its fallen brethren would be rank now, and that there was no reason to feast on the fallen. Others would be, it knew, but there would always be the scavengers and the desperate.

It sniffed, drawing in the scent of the ones that had got away. Two had been infected, and that was good. But they had been taken, and in a craft. That meant they travelled far.

It reached out, and the trail of the craft hung in the air, despite the downpour. It turned, facing the way the craft had gone.

The infected, and the others, had run because they were frightened. But they had been organised. They had managed to exploit a weakness, and so they were not unintelligent. And that meant they were not running blind. They would be seeking safety.

It called out, reaching for its brethren, and many responded. Not all, but that was no problem. There would always be stragglers. They would understand in time.

It jumped from the branch and landed on the soft ground, in the midst of its brethren. It stretched upright, uttered a rallying cry and pulled in more attention.

The craft could be followed, and the brethren were strong. They could feed on the forest beasts if required, or take sustenance from their weaker kin. But they could track their quarry.

The quarry ran to safety. There was safety in numbers.

And that meant more opportunities to feed.

The story of *Shadows* continues in

Shadowsiege (Shadows Book Two)

Not all monsters hide in shadows.

Ryann should feel safe, but everything has changed. Haven is under siege from the shades. They hide in the shadows of the forest, waiting for night, always hungry.

But they don't always kill. Sometimes, their bite infects.

Cathal lies in quarantine, the infection changing his body, turning him into something else. He sleeps, as do the other infected —but sooner or later, they will wake.

Then there are the men from the company. They say they have come down to Haven in order to help, but as far as Ryann can tell, they are only helping themselves. And in a company this big, individuals are of no consequence.

Whichever way she turns, Ryann is besieged by monster.

A NOTE FROM TW IAIN

Thank you for reading *Shadowfall*.

Brice and the others might be heading back to the safety of Haven, but the story is not yet over, and there are many questions as yet unanswered. In *Shadowsiege*, find out what happens back at the base, discover what happens to Cathal, and learn more about the origins of the creatures. And the story concludes in *Shadowstrike*.

But what about the missing crew at the beginning of *Shadowfall*? Their story is told in the novella *Shadowlair*, and the only way to get hold of this e-book is by joining my newsletter list. I e-mail subscribers roughly once a month with news of upcoming releases, books I've read that you might enjoy, as well as more free books. Sign up by visiting bit.ly/TWI_list.

I'd love to know what you think of *Shadowfall* (or any of my other stories). You can contact me at twiain@twiain.com, or alternatively you can leave a review on Amazon or Goodreads (or anywhere else). For an independently-published author, reviews are important, because they let others know more about the book. And I appreciate any feedback.

Thank you.

TW Iain

Printed in Great Britain
by Amazon

24819437R00129